CAPTURED
in the
CARIBBEAN

Captured in the Caribbean

Copyright © 2015 by Sara Whitford

First Edition.
ISBN-13: 978-0-9863252-1-2
ISBN-10: 0-9863252-1-X

Copy edited by Marcus Trower.

www.adamfletcherseries.com
www.sarawhitford.com

SEAPORT
PUBLISHING

Printed in the U.S.A

FOR ISAAC

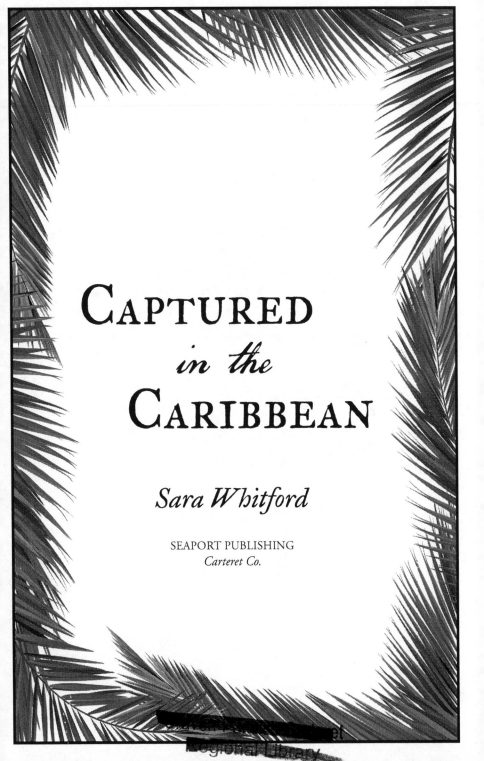

Captured
in the
Caribbean

Sara Whitford

SEAPORT PUBLISHING
Carteret Co.

Chapter One

June 1766—somewhere off the coast of the Bahamas

"BETTER REPENT NOW, boys, and get your souls in order," said Captain Carl Phillips, laughing as he observed his sorry-looking crew. "If you think it's hot now, just imagine what Hell will be like."

Adam Fletcher wanted to chuckle. In fact, the dark-haired eighteen-year-old tried, but the best he could do in the stifling heat on board the deck of the *Carolina Gypsy* was to mop the sweat off of his face and from around the back of his neck with his handkerchief and let out a little "Heh!" as he looked over at his friend Martin, who was equally miserable.

"Damned doldrums," said Charlie Phillips, the ship's mate and younger brother of the captain as he leaned back against the rail and looked up at the mast, as though if he watched the sails long enough they would begin to move.

For two days the sixty-ton Bermuda sloop had been stalled somewhere east of Nassau in windless seas.

The blond-haired, ruddy-complected Captain Phillips was an experienced sailor who had spent plenty of time sitting under a scorching sun in still ocean waters, as had his younger brother, Charlie, who at age twenty-four was about eight years his junior.

The Phillipses were from a long seafaring tradition. In fact, their father and all of their uncles had been sailors and sailmakers. And as was the case with all of the men employed by Rogers's Shipping Company, the Phillipses had a personal connection to Emmanuel Rogers. In their case, their grandfather and one of their uncles had sailed with Emmanuel during his pirating days.

There were only seven men aboard the *Gypsy* for this trip: Captain Carl Phillips; Mate Charlie Phillips; three regular seamen—Fred Canady, Ed Willis, and Ricky Jones; a cooper, Martin Smith; and the cooper's apprentice, Adam. Their final destination was Havana, but first they had to make a stop in Nassau before continuing to sail south and then west towards Havana.

Captain Phillips didn't seem fazed by the stifling heat of the windless seas, but Charlie, who had an anxious disposition, never had gotten used to it. For Adam and Martin, however, it was their first time passing through anything like it.

"Hey, Cap'n," said Adam. "What's the longest stretch you've spent without moving like this?"

Captain Phillips pressed his lips together pensively, then grinned and said, "About a week, I reckon."

Charlie, who was the spitting image of his older brother,

only thinner, studied him for a minute, then said, "When? I don't remember us ever bein stuck out like this for a week."

Carl laughed. "Maybe you haven't but I have, when you was a little thing."

Charlie rolled his eyes to express his doubt.

Martin made no effort to hide his skepticism. "When was it, then, that you were stuck like this for a week?"

"One of the first times I went out on the *Gypsy*—'bout twelve years ago. Abner Blake was the captain then. And I didn't say we was stuck for a week. I said it was *about* a week. We took her to Bermuda, and we went through one stretch where we were stuck in irons in seas that looked like a lake."

"Were you scared?" asked Adam.

The captain nodded his head low and said, "What do you think?" He laughed. "Damn right I was scared! I thought we was all gonna get cooked under the hot sun. 'Twas even worse than the sun we're under now, bein it was the middle of August then rather than the start of June."

Martin pulled off the cloth he'd tied around his head to keep his sandy curls off of his face and used it to wipe his brow. "What about you, Adam? You scared now?"

Adam rolled his eyes at his friend and gave a dismissive "Tsk!" He said, "Well, it's hot. I'm sweating like a pig, and I won't say that I haven't considered the possibility we might die out here, but no, I'm not scared. Mostly just impatient. How 'bout you? You scared?"

Martin wrinkled his brow and chuckled. "No." He swallowed hard and said, "Of course not."

"I'm just ready to get to Havana . . . Get this cargo unloaded and have a few hours of shore leave so I can take care of *my* business."

"Good Lord, boy!" came an unmistakable twangy voice. Adam knew who it was, but he still turned around to see that it was indeed Fred Canady. The straw-haired thirtysomething-year-old was coming up the ladder from below deck after disappearing for about twenty minutes to go to the head. "I reckon we'll all be glad to get to Havana, so we can stop hearin you go on and on about *your* business," Canady said.

"Right. Because your endless stories about all those *friendly* women who you find in every port are so much more interesting to listen to. To listen to things the way you tell 'em, it's a wonder you aren't dead from some kind of pox," Adam remarked, laughing.

Canady tipped his head and slyly cocked his eyebrow. "Guess I'm just lucky," he said.

"Or full of bilge," said Martin. "Have you looked in a mirror lately?" he asked. "I've seen oysters that are better lookin! I reckon any woman goin home with you would expect payment in advance."

The others all howled with laughter.

"It's my dazzlin personality they love," quipped Canady, unembarrassed. "We can't all be as handsome as you, Smith."

Cocky as ever, Martin stroked his chiseled, stubbly face and flashed his blue eyes. "No, I don't reckon you can."

The banter was all in good fun. Fred Canady was without question a rough-looking man. He was one of those people whose face looked angry all the time, in spite of the fact that he was a joker at heart. Martin Smith, on the other hand, was known throughout Carteret County as an unabashed Casanova. In fact, he'd once even tried to work his charms on Adam Fletcher's thirty-five-year-old mother, but much to Adam's relief she had the good sense to be unmoved by Martin's advances.

It was a wonder the two had become such good friends, but at twenty-six, Martin was the youngest cooper at Rogers's Shipping Company, and in the year since Adam had been bound apprentice to Emmanuel Rogers, Martin had become like a big brother to him.

The previous spring, when Adam had first learned he and Martin would be traveling to Havana on board Emmanuel's sloop as the ship's coopers, he could barely contain his excitement. His mother, Mary, on the other hand, fell apart when she learned he'd be making the trip. After all, she'd just gotten over nearly losing him at the hands of a nefarious plot by another local merchant. In an effort to calm Mary's nerves, Emmanuel promised her he would wait and send Adam the following spring—after his eighteenth birthday—rather than having him go on the autumn trip, and Martin assured her that he, along with the whole crew of the *Gypsy*, would look after Adam and make sure to bring him back in one piece. Everyone knew she was not at all happy about the situation, but she acknowledged that it was a small comfort knowing everyone would be looking out for him, and said she'd hold Martin and Emmanuel personally responsible if anything happened to her son on the voyage. Her threat had no teeth, as there was nothing she could've done if something did happen to Adam, but they all thought so highly of Mary that no one wanted to disappoint her.

THE SUN WAS ABOUT to set when tall and lanky Ed Willis, a blond-haired twentysomething, announced, "Look! The topsail!" He pointed up the mast as a gentle breeze was causing the uppermost sail on the vessel to begin to flap. Just as the men all looked up to see it, the jib and mainsail began to puff up and fill with wind. The men, who for the most part were hardly religious, cheered and were nevertheless thanking God for getting them moving again.

Within hours, though, their joy turned to new fear as they moved from fair winds into a violent storm. The men were being pelted with fast and heavy rain that came down in sheets, so much that they could barely see. Their foul weather coats—at least they might be called that—were made of canvas that had been waterproofed with a coat of tar, but they could do little to help keep them dry in the current conditions.

"Are we in a hurricane, Cap'n?" Adam yelled over the noisy torrent.

"Not this one, Mr. Fletcher," he shouted back. "I reckon it's just a squall. Makes no difference, though! We have to push through it either way."

Adam nodded. "Yes, sir."

None of the men slept that night, as they all had their positions on deck tending the sails and the lines.

Chapter Two

AFTER ABOUT TEN days spent either in irons in the windless seas east of Nassau or doing their best to push through a summer squall, they finally limped into port at Havana's harbor. A pilot boat came out to meet their vessel and then guided them to the dock at the warehouse where they would be delivering their cargo. It was on the edge of the main harbor, so they could see much of what was happening there.

Adam was energetic and eager to moor the vessel and get the cargo off-loaded. He knew that as soon as they did, they could find out what more would need to be done before they'd get their shore leave. Considering they were on such a tight schedule, being afforded free time after moving cargo was a luxury the crew didn't typically get. However, since Mr. Gomez, the merchant to whom they were delivering the goods, was another of Emmanuel's old friends, he usually offered to entertain Emmanuel's men while they were in port. The old merchant was traveling this time, but nevertheless the offer was always open to allow the *Gypsy* to dock there a day or two so that the men would have a chance to get a meal in town and to perform any necessary maintenance or repairs on the vessel.

This time it might even take longer than a day, as the headstay had frayed after that storm east of Nassau. It might take a couple of days to repair.

While Adam had made a few short jaunts to ports in closer proximity to Beaufort, he had never seen anything like the harbor in Havana. There were ships of every size and design from all over the world. Some were fitted out for trade, others looked as if they were ready for war. Many were either receiving or sending out lighters—smaller, flat-bottomed boats that were more able to navigate the waters between the large vessels and the docks.

The busy wharf was packed with people—some were no doubt sailors moving to and from their vessels, while others were locals who appeared to be either doing business in the wharf or just observing the wares being brought into their port.

As they moved into their position outside the warehouse, Adam began to see what was attracting a large contingent of the crowd on the docks about fifty yards farther down the harbor. It was something he had never seen before in North Carolina, but he knew immediately what it was. The schooner, which looked to be over a hundred feet long, was a slaver. There were already about two dozen Africans clustered on the docks down there, and they were being inspected by several men. Probably about a hundred more could be seen lined up on the deck of the ship, while still others were being brought between the schooner and the dock on a lighter.

Neither Adam nor Martin had even laid eyes on a slave

ship before, so they couldn't help but rest against the rail and stare. North Carolina did not have ports that were particularly suitable for the kinds of vessels that carried human cargo. There were slaves back home, to be sure—usually brought into the colony from Virginia or South Carolina—but in a little town like Beaufort, there were no big plantations to speak of, and the slaves that did live and work there seemed to be very different than the Negros Adam saw coming off of that ship. For one thing these poor souls were stark naked and chained together, either in pairs (if they were women or children) or in groups of five or six (if they were men). Adam had only ever seen slaves wearing English-style clothing, and all of the ones he knew personally also spoke English. He could tell by the frightened expressions on the faces of these shackled Africans, however, that they were entirely incapable of understanding what the men who were examining them were saying. The inspectors appeared to be looking over each one the way he'd seen farmers do with livestock back home—to make sure they were fit and healthy before finalizing their purchase. As some of the slaves passed through their inspections, they were taken by men who were standing nearby with papers in hand, presumably bills of sale.

As a column of women and children were led onto the docks, Adam averted his eyes. He had never seen a naked woman before—at least not since he'd been old enough to understand what they were. He wondered if the females were as embarrassed to be naked before all of these men as he felt seeing their dark-brown, womanly frames paraded down onto the docks to be inspected.

Adam and Martin exchanged melancholy glances.

Charlie must have noticed them and said, "You two have never seen one of those before, huh?"

"No," said Adam.

Martin shook his head.

"It's a real busy industry," said Charlie. "Folks got to get their help from somewhere, I reckon."

Adam wrinkled his brow but said nothing. He could tell from the way Charlie had said what he did that he was not at all impressed with the business. Adam was reminded of a conversation he once had with Emmanuel about his days pirating with Blackbeard—and how seeing the actual conditions on the slave ship *La Concorde* left him detesting the industry. While Adam had not had the same up-close experience that Emmanuel had, it was enough for him to see what his master had found so revolting.

ADAM PROBABLY WORKED HARDER than anyone else unloading the *Gypsy* that day. *Somewhere in this busy town,* he thought, *I might finally find the man who can tell me something about my father. The sooner we can get this job done, the sooner I can go looking for him.* He was annoyed to see one of his shipmates, Ricky Jones, milling around on the docks talking to some local men while everyone else was busy lifting barrels of turpentine, rosin, and other commodities up onto the deck to be off-loaded.

"Who's he talking to and why?" Adam asked Captain Phillips. "He ought to be up here working with the rest of us!"

The captain looked down from the bow onto the docks, and when he saw it was Jones, he rolled his eyes and yelled at the idler. "Hey! Jones! Hurry up and get your ass back on deck and get to work! You can do that later!"

"Be right there, Cap'n!" Jones called out. He exchanged a few more words with the mustachioed Spaniard on the docks and then sprinted up the ramp to rejoin his shipmates on board.

"What were you doin down there?" asked Martin.

"Findin us a place to have a drink tonight, mate," Jones responded. If it weren't for his Yorkshire accent, the dark-haired, brown-eyed young sailor could've easily passed for Adam's brother. As long as anyone in Emmanuel Rogers's company had known him, he'd made it a point of seeking out the favorite local taverns wherever the *Gypsy* made port. While he was perfectly content to drink alone, he was always looking for opportunities to imbibe socially.

"I'm sure there are plenty of taverns around. You felt like you needed to ask a local?" asked Adam.

"Unfortunately, the last time we were in Havana," said Jones, "some of our good shipmates had a few too many at our previous waterin place . . . and there was this big fight and there were arrests. The whole thing was an ugly affair, so I had to find us someplace new."

As he got back to work helping his shipmates, Martin asked him, "Well, did you find one?"

Jones nodded. "Course I did." He helped Adam lift a cask of turpentine up onto the ramp from the deck of the ship and then roll it down to the docks. "And you'll be happy to learn it'll be a free round at that."

"How did you manage that?" Martin called down the ramp from behind him as he and Charlie followed the same procedure.

"Actually, we can thank young Mr. Fletcher here," said Jones.

As they got down to the dock and rolled the barrel to the holding area, Adam gave him a confused look and said, "What?"

"It's the truth! That chap I was talkin to said he had been watchin us since we arrived. He asked who you were—said that you looked like you were workin so hard. He asked if you always worked like this."

Adam laughed. "What'd you tell him?" he asked, out of breath.

"I told him 'Of course not!'" said Jones as they proceeded back up the ramp to get another barrel. "Told him you're the laziest one in the lot, but that you're tryin to win a wager."

"Oh, thank you!" said Adam facetiously.

"Anytime, mate," said Jones with a chuckle.

They boarded the ship again and went over to the area where the men were pulling up cargo from the ship's hold to the deck, and they selected another barrel and repeated the process.

"I'm just joking, mate. I told him you're in a hurry to have your shore leave."

Adam nodded. "Well, that's true. I am that."

OFF-LOADING THE CARGO FROM the *Gypsy* took a lot longer than Adam expected. Then again he really didn't have much of a basis for comparison. All of his experience with moving goods from off a vessel was either at Emmanuel's warehouse, where the loading area was part of the building's structure, or Emmanuel's second dock at Laney Martin's estate, and that one was used only rarely—when Emmanuel received merchandise from the French or Spanish West Indies, and these were usually much smaller shipments. The docks for this warehouse were much longer and extended much farther out in the water, so they had a greater distance to go to deliver the goods.

The sun was going down and the men were ravenous. The crew members all decided to go to the tavern that Jones had learned about from the local man.

The place was called Taberna El Trobador. The aptly named establishment was known in Havana as the best place to hear popular traveling musicians. On this night the men from the *Gypsy* were not disappointed. There were, in fact, two musicians performing together—one playing a guitar, and the other clapping a pair of castanets, keeping rhythm while stomping his foot occasionally for emphasis. Carl and Charlie Phillips had heard the fiery style of music before, as had Jones and the others who had been to Havana, but for Adam and Martin it was an entirely new experience.

They took some tables near the tavern's entrance—something Captain Phillips had put into practice ages ago. As he said, "Ya never know when all hell will break loose in these kinds of places, so best you stay near the door in case you need to make a quick escape."

The furnishings were all made of heavy mahogany, and the architectural details were quite different from what would ordinarily be found in Beaufort. By the light of the lamps that illuminated the place, the plaster walls looked like they were a dark, mossy green. As Adam looked around and took in every inch of the exotic tavern, he observed vibrant objects in nearly every nook and cranny. There were deep-red and gold-colored objects everywhere, such as brass sconces with cranberry-tinted glass on the walls. Behind the stage area where the musicians performed hung a wine-colored tapestry. It wasn't actually a stage, though, but rather just a cleared area along the building's northern wall.

Adam was intoxicated by the atmosphere and could not help but tap his feet in time to the song. Martin, on the other hand, appeared to be taking in the sights—specifically the young Spanish women who seemed like they were right at home in the place, and perhaps even more importantly, who looked adept at making the patrons feel right at home as well.

Soon, a tall, thin waiter who appeared to be about Adam's age came to the table to take the order. Captain Phillips responded in Spanish colored with the thick brogue that was typical of the barrier island families on the Carolina coast. The waiter looked like he struggled to understand him, but in the end he nodded and disappeared into the crowd so he could fill the order.

Charlie asked his older brother, "What'd you tell him?"

"I reckoned I best keep it simple." He grinned. "Told him beers all around and whatever he recommends for supper."

About that time the mustachioed man from the docks—a fellow of about fiftysomething years of age—came in flanked by two other men who looked about half his age.

Charlie, who was sitting facing the entrance, kicked Jones under the table and then tipped his head towards the door.

Jones turned around and waved at the man and his friends as soon as he spotted them. "Hello, mate!" he shouted over the sound of the musicians.

The man motioned for his companions to go on over to the next table and to have a seat.

"Have you gentlemen already asked for your drinks?" asked the Spaniard.

"Aye, indeed we have, sir," said Jones.

"I will tell the waiter to put this round on my account."

Jones and the rest of the Gypsy crew who were present all cheered and told him thank you.

He walked around the tables where the crew sat and joined his companions at the table they had chosen nearby. It was closest to where Adam and Martin were seated.

Adam turned his chair sideways so he could talk to him. "You speak English very well, sir."

The man pulled out a chair and took a seat. "Thank you, young man. I suppose one could say it is necessary in my work."

Adam noticed he was dressed quite well and wondered about his occupation. "What do you do?"

The man smiled and appeared as though he might be studying Adam's face before he answered. "I am—how do you call it?—the high sheriff."

Adam unintentionally swallowed hard, which he was sure made him look suspicious. "Oh, really? Of all of Havana?"

The man nodded.

"So I reckon that means you're the law here, huh?"

The man tipped his head from side to side and gave a little grin. "I do not make the laws, but let us say that it is my job to enforce them."

Adam suddenly felt nervous, though he didn't know why. He hadn't done anything wrong . . . not personally, anyway. Of course earlier in the day he and the crew had smuggled several hundred pounds of commodities into Mr. Gomez's warehouse, but that was for Spanish customs to worry about, not the sheriff—at least that's the way he understood things to work. When it came down to it, there was no reason for him to have any problems with the law.

He began to wonder if the man might be wanting to keep an eye on him and his shipmates because of some of the trouble Jones said the crew of the *Gypsy* had gotten into the previous year. He thought it might be wise to change the subject and ask the man about something else.

"I reckon you must've lived here a long time—I mean, you know a lot of people, right?"

Just then the waiter came and brought drinks to Adam and the men at his table. He looked over at the sheriff and his friends and said, "*¿Su orden habitual, señor?*"

The mustachioed man nodded and said something in Spanish, and then the waiter left to fetch more drinks. The sheriff turned his attention back to Adam and said, "I was born here in Havana, so of course I know many people in this place."

"Hmph." Adam thought for a moment. "Maybe you can help me then."

"What is it you are needing help about?"

"Have you ever heard of a man called Alonso Cordova? He was a sailor."

"Hmm . . . I do not believe so. As a matter of fact, I do not know anyone here who has the name Cordova now that I am thinking about it."

Adam was visibly disappointed.

"You are looking for this man? Is he someone you know?"

"No, not exactly. But I heard he lives here and that he might know about someone that I am looking for."

"Ah." The man nodded. "I understand. I only wish I could be of more help to you."

"That's alright," said Adam. "I'll try to ask around some in town tomorrow. My friend here has promised to come with me." He elbowed Martin to indicate who he was talking about, but when he turned to look at his friend, he noticed Martin was whispering in the ear of a young woman who had just pulled up a chair right next to him. Adam rolled his eyes.

The mustachioed man said something to the girl in Spanish, to which she responded.

The man told Adam, "She really likes your friend."

"All the girls do. Back home folks lock up their daughters when they see Martin coming down the street." He laughed.

The man grinned. "Your friend is enjoying some of our local hospitality. This is good. You should have a nice time here so you will go back to your home with many pleasant memories."

Adam looked over at Martin and the Spanish girl, then shook his head and chuckled. "No, sir. I have a girl back home. I reckon I'll have a nice time here, but not quite like my friend."

The man laughed. "I suppose your home is very far away from here, yes?"

Adam nodded. "Yes, sir. We're here all the way from Beaufort, North Carolina."

"Ah! Well, you see, that is very far! It is not necessary that your señorita knows everything you do while you are away."

"Perhaps," Adam shrugged, "but all the same my heart belongs to her."

"Ay, ay, ay! To be young and so innocent! You should know that you do not need to involve your heart to have a good time. It is only a bit of fun and diversion." The man laughed loudly, but when Adam failed to laugh along, he said, "Nevertheless, I suppose it is virtuous that you are a faithful man."

Adam wrinkled his brow. He wasn't sure how to respond. Back in Beaufort you'd never hear a man of power and means bragging about infidelity right out in public. Adam didn't know if it was the culture of a busy port city that made the man that way, or if it was just a Spanish characteristic. He suspected a little of both. He had heard it said that people of Mediterranean descent tended to be hot-blooded. Then again a lot of folks back home would've said that Martin was hot-blooded, but as much of a womanizer as he was, even he wouldn't carry on a serious relationship with one woman while having another on the side. That's precisely why at twenty-six, Martin Smith still hadn't even considered settling down with one woman yet. He knew he couldn't commit to just one girl, so he never did.

At that point things became a little awkward between Adam and the sheriff, so Adam directed his attention back towards listening to the musicians, and the man turned his focus to Jones, who had come around from his table and taken a seat at the table with the sheriff. Soon the two of them were engaged in an animated conversation, much to Adam's relief. He wasn't sure how to converse with the man without possibly offending him, and considering he held such a position of authority, that was the last thing he wanted to do.

Within a few minutes the waiter and a couple of assistants from the kitchen came out to deliver the food that had been ordered—the special that the captain had mentioned. The crew members were surprised to be served roasted pork that was remarkably similar to their pit-cooked barbecue pork back home. This must've been the dish that Emmanuel had told Adam about. He had once explained to his apprentice that the North Carolina way of cooking barbecue pork had been brought to the American colonies from the Caribbean. Of course Adam hadn't seen a recipe for either method, but from what he could tell, the main difference seemed to be that the Cuban pork tasted like some sort of citrus juice was being used in place of the vinegar that was added to the pork back home. There were no vegetables— something that would've always been served with supper at the Topsail Tavern. Instead, they were presented with a dish that Adam learned was called Moros y Cristianos. It was apparently just a fancy name for black beans and rice. Everything was put on the table in large platters so that the men might serve themselves.

There were some condiments served alongside that Adam did not recognize, but he was eager to try them all the same.

After the meal was done, Adam elbowed Martin. "Hey you—are you going to stay here much longer?"

Martin raised his eyebrows at him, then turned his attention back to the Spanish girl, who at this point was sitting on his lap. He leaned over and whispered something to her. She whispered something back.

Adam wondered what they could possibly be saying, given Martin's limited command of the Spanish language. When the girl kissed Martin on the cheek and began to twine her fingers in his sandy curls, Adam knew it was unlikely he'd see his friend again that night.

"Listen," he told him, "I'm going back to the *Gypsy*. I'll see you in the morning at eight, and we can go to the plaza and start asking around."

Martin nodded and answered Adam while keeping his eyes on the girl. "That sounds like a real good plan."

Adam and the captain—the only two who weren't being entertained by local women—decided to head back to the ship.

Chapter Three

ADAM SMOOTHED HIS dark, wavy hair back from out of his face and fastened it with a cord in a short ponytail. The choppy wind blowing across the deck of the *Gypsy* at his back made him glad they weren't at sea that day. He'd been leaning on the ship's rail on and off for nearly an hour on the lookout for his friend when he pulled out his pocket watch to check the time. *This is ridiculous*, he thought as he closed his watch and shoved it back in his pocket.

Martin still hadn't shown up, and it was nearly nine o'clock already. He had agreed the previous evening to meet Adam at eight, and then they would go to the Plaza Vieja, the old market square near the wharf, to ask around about Alonso Cordova.

Adam didn't have to think too hard about where his friend was. Martin always struggled with punctuality where women were concerned. *Forget about this! I'm not waiting all day for him to fasten his britches and meet me here.*

Adam had known better than to expect him to return to the sloop the previous night, but he expected his friend would at least come dragging in shortly after sunup. The fact that it was now nearly nine o'clock and he was apparently still with his señorita meant there was no telling when he'd turn up again. It could be anytime before nightfall, when Captain Phillips would do a check to make sure all of the men were back on board so that he could be sure they'd all be ready to work at sunup the next day.

He decided he would head to the Plaza Vieja himself. He told Jones where he was going and asked if he would like to tag along.

"Wish I could, mate," he said, "but the cap'n is sending me and Canady out to try and track down some line so we can replace that frayed headstay."

"Well, I reckon I should be back in a few hours. I don't know how much success I'll have looking for that Cordova man, since I don't speak Spanish."

"Ah, well, good luck, mate," said Jones. "If Smith gets back before I leave, I'll tell him where he can find you."

Adam nodded and took off for the plaza.

He didn't have to walk very far to get there. The place was only about two blocks west of the docks. As soon as he came through the northeastern entrance, Adam found it to be a pleasant assault on his senses. Vendors with stalls set up in this market square in the heart of downtown Havana offered the same sort of things that would have been sold in any city market in America, but with a decidedly Cuban flavor. The colorful wares and exotic produce marked a departure from the merchandise to which Adam had grown accustomed back in Beaufort. Noisy vendors walked around with baskets on their heads full of freshly baked breads and pastries, while others hawked peanuts or fritters.

The pungent but appetizing aromas wafting out of one of the local cafés, which Adam remembered were called *fondas*, stimulated his taste buds and finally enticed him to spend some of his hard-earned money on foods he did not know how to name. He enjoyed eating at one of the tables on the patio in front of the place while he stayed on the lookout, just in case Martin turned up.

After his belly was full, he went to check the northeastern gate one last time for his friend.

Where is he? Adam was frustrated. He hadn't wanted to go on this mission alone, but now it looked like he would have to. After all, the *Gypsy* was scheduled to leave port to start on the return trip to Beaufort in less than twenty-four hours. And since they were all to be back on board by nightfall, he now had only a handful of hours to accomplish his task.

What was already a long shot now seemed to be nearing impossible. In a city as busy as Havana, where they didn't generally speak English, Adam wondered how he was ever going to find the only person who might be able to tell him something about his father. At least Martin knew a little bit of Spanish, unlike Adam, who only knew how to say things like *hola, gracias, no hablo español,* and *adios.*

Before he had left Beaufort, Valentine Hodges, proprietor of the Topsail Tavern and Adam's surrogate grandfather (by virtue of having raised his mother, Mary, since she was a young girl), had told him when he got to Havana to try to find a man called Alonso Cordova, also known as Poncho. As much as Valentine would've liked to, he didn't have any more information that he could share with the boy. He had promised Mary when Adam was born that he would never tell him who his father was, and he intended to keep that promise.

However, Mary had never thought to issue such a prohibition about him telling Adam the name of the man who had been his father's best friend and shipmate when the young captain had spent time in Beaufort all those years ago, so that's exactly what Valentine did.

Adam had mentioned the name to the waiter at the *fonda*, but he shrugged and shook his head. He was fairly certain that meant the waiter didn't know anyone by that name, but it also could have meant he simply didn't understand what he was saying. Adam decided a better course of action would be to try to find someone who could speak both English and Spanish.

He started by asking a vendor at one of the stalls selling produce. "Excuse me, señor. Do you speak English?"

The old man wrinkled his eyebrows and gave Adam a confused look.

Adam opted for the one-word approach. "English? *¿Inglés?*"

The man shook his head and walked away. Adam assumed it was because the vendor had figured out he wasn't a customer.

Adam looked around and spotted a crowd of men milling around in front of the entrance to what looked like it could be an inn. He wondered if he might find an interpreter there. As he got closer to where the men were standing outside talking, he realized they weren't speaking Spanish or English. In fact, he had no idea what language they were speaking. He'd never heard it before. Nevertheless, he knew Havana was a busy port, so they could be sailors from anywhere. If they were able to communicate with the staff well enough to rent rooms in that establishment, maybe there would be someone inside who could help him.

He went in and spoke to a man standing behind a counter there. "Excuse me, but I'm looking for someone who speaks English."

The man shrugged and shook his head.

Dejected, Adam left the building and began approaching anyone who was working in the plaza to see if they were able to speak English.

As he went around the marketplace hoping to find someone who might be able to help him, a man began following him at some distance. He was a Spaniard of average height—just slightly shorter than Adam—and had a stocky build. He had very curly black hair, which he kept pulled back in a ponytail, and a stubbly face.

He made his way over to Adam and introduced himself. "¡*Hola, amigo!* It seems you . . . ah . . . needing help."

Adam's eyes grew wide. "You speak English! And Spanish! Oh, thank God! I've been trying to find someone who can help me."

"Yes, I speaking English and Espanish," said the man. "For what you needing help?"

"I'm trying to find a man who lives here in Havana—at least he did many years ago. He was a sailor."

"*Ay, hombre* . . . there are many sailors living in Havana, señor. How do you call him?"

Adam wrinkled his brow. "How do I—?"

"His name. How do you calling his name?"

"Oh, well, his name is Alonso Cordova."

The man stood there and appeared to be thinking about whether or not the name was familiar to him. Finally, he spoke. "I knowing a man called Alonso, and I know a *familia* called Cordova, but I not knowing a man called Alonso Cordova."

Adam sighed. "Hmm. Well, do you think anybody in that family might know him? I mean, could they be related?"

"Wait a minute . . . *Dejame pensar un momento* . . ." The man scratched at his stubbly cheeks as he thought for a moment. "You say Alonso, yes?"

Adam wasn't sure what he had said, but he heard the word "Alonso" in there, so he nodded, then said, "Yes, Alonso Cordova."

"You not knowing if he might be having other name, like Poncho, yes?"

Adam's face lit up. "Poncho! Yes, Poncho! His nickname was Poncho! Do you know him?"

The man smiled. "Ah, I not knowing him myself, but I knowing who he is. He is a . . ." He searched for the word. "How you saying the word *primo*? . . . Cousin? Yes? Yes, he is a cousin of this family Cordova that I telling you about."

Adam smiled broadly. "Can you take me to him? Or at least to this family?"

The man hemmed and hawed.

"I'll pay you!"

The man raised his eyebrows. Adam could tell his offer interested him.

"Listen, I have to find this man before nightfall. If they get our ship's repairs done in time, we'll be leaving at sunup. I have to find this man and talk to him so I can be back before curfew."

"What you wanting with this man?"

Adam wasn't about to tell this stranger he was looking for his father. He figured the man might be reluctant to get involved in something of that nature. Instead, he told him, "My grandfather said he knew him. Said I should look for him, since I'll be in Havana."

The man smiled. "I understand. I can take you to the house of the *familia* Cordova, but they living outside of this town. It is about an hour walking. But I thinking they can tell you where you finding this Poncho that you seek."

"An hour?" Adam took out his pocket watch to check the time, then thought for a moment. "Could we hire someone to take us? Like a carriage?"

"*Claro*, but it costing you more."

Adam gave the man two coins. "How about if I pay you these now? You get us a driver and help me talk to this Cordova family. If we can find Poncho, I'll pay you five more of these when you bring me back here tonight. If we don't find Poncho, I'll pay you two more. Does that sound fair?"

"This is fine," said the man. "I knowing a man with a horse who can taking us."

Adam was relieved but anxious. As he followed his newly hired interpreter, it occurred to him that they hadn't been properly introduced. "What's your name?" he asked.

"I am called Hector. *¿Y Usted?* How you calling yourself?"

"My name is Adam. Adam Fletcher."

They crossed over to the southwestern entrance of the plaza and exited. As soon as they were outside, the man approached a fellow feeding his horse out by the hitching posts. He had a small, simple cart—the kind that a farmer would use to bring his produce to the market.

"*¡Oye, hombre!*" said Hector.

"*¿Cómo estás, amigo?*" said the fellow feeding his horse. He was a very tall, thin man with long, greasy, salt and pepper hair and green eyes.

The two men began to speak rapidly in Spanish. Adam didn't understand any of it except for the words "Cordova," "Adam Fletcher," and *dinero*. He figured even if he couldn't understand exactly what they were saying, Hector must be explaining what the situation was.

The tall man's green eyes grew large, and then he laughed and nodded. Hector told Adam they had struck a deal on the price and would take him directly to see the Cordova family.

Soon they were on their way.

Chapter Four

"OY, MATE!" SAID Jones as he saw Martin Smith making his way slowly up the ramp of the *Gypsy*. "It's about time your sorry ass turned up. A bit late in the day, don't you think?"

Martin grabbed at his head as he stepped on deck and raised up his other palm to shush Jones. "Don't yell. My head is poundin."

"Serves you right. Fletcher waited here for you until about nine, then took off. Got tired of hangin around."

Martin leaned against the rail. "What? He's already gone?" He looked up at the sky, but it was too bright, so he squinted his eyes painfully and asked, "What time is it, anyway?"

"It's about noon, mate."

Martin was slow to respond but was clearly stunned. He wrinkled his brow. "You're jokin. It's really that late?"

"Yes, it is. What'd you get up to last night, anyway? You look like hell."

"I went off with that girl . . . Was having a pretty good time, too, and then I passed out, I reckon." He grabbed at his head again, then stretched his neck from side to side and front to back in an effort to get some relief. "I wonder if she put something in that wine."

Jones shrugged. "Who knows?" He chuckled. "Heh. Never had a girl do that before."

"Me neither." He leaned over the rail and inhaled deeply in an effort to get some fresh air into his lungs. "Don't know why she'd do something like that, anyway. I was completely willing *and* able."

Jones rolled his eyes. "You idiot! Have you checked your pockets?"

Martin's eyes grew wide. He quickly thrust his hands into his pockets but found that none of his money had been stolen. He knew she was a "woman of the town," and although he had never been asked to pay for companionship, he was still fully prepared to give her a coin or two before he left if she asked.

She must have really liked him, he thought.

"How long ago did Fletcher leave?"

"I told you," said Jones, "he left about nine."

"This is very bad. Very, very bad," said Martin as he started to pace back and forth on the deck.

Just then Charlie boarded the vessel. "What are you two rascals up to?"

"Smith pulled one on last night. Now he's having a fit because Fletcher's gone off without him."

"Fletcher left already? Where'd he go?" asked Charlie.

"Said he was going to the Plaza Vieja. He and Smith were

supposed to have gone there this morning, but Fletcher got tired of waiting around," said Jones. "I don't reckon it would have made much of a difference if he had been here on time. He's in a right state, this one." He tipped his head towards Martin.

Charlie leaned his tall, slender frame against the mast and watched his shipmate. "I sure hope that little señorita was worth it. You better pray Adam don't get lost out there wanderin around Havana. It ain't like he speaks any Spanish."

He and Jones laughed heartily.

"You two laugh. This ain't funny, though. This is bad . . . really, really bad." Martin kicked at the ground and growled in frustration.

Jones wrinkled his brow, as though he couldn't understand why Martin was reacting so badly. "You're takin this kind of hard, mate. What's the problem? Afraid he's goin to have a good time or something?"

"Settle down, Smith," said Charlie. "He'll be back by tonight. He has to be. My brother's doing a head count at nightfall."

"Well, I'm not waiting around here until tonight to see if he turns up. I've got to go find him . . . I swanny! That boy is so damned impatient. Why didn't y'all tell him to wait for me?"

"Why should he have to wait around for you?" asked Jones. "You said you'd meet him at eight. You weren't here. He gave up on you at nine. It's noon now. Speakin o'which, I better go. I told that rope maker I'd be back at his shop before one to pick up the lines for our repairs."

He excused himself and left the *Gypsy* to head into town.

"He's right," said Charlie. "This is no cause for concern. We've all got a bit of freedom until tonight. No reason Adam shouldn't be able to enjoy it."

"You don't understand," said Martin. "You don't know him like I do. He's never been on one of these trips before. He's Emmanuel's responsibility, since he's barely eighteen and still an apprentice. Emmanuel specifically made him *my* responsibility on this trip. If we end up losin him here in Havana, how do you think that will go when we get back to Beaufort?"

"Lose him?" Charlie scoffed at the notion. "He's not a child, Martin. Anyway, you knew this was important to him. You can't expect that he'd wait around for you all day. He's been runnin his mouth constantly about looking for this man ever since he knew we'd be makin the trip. And you know how he is. He ain't one for waitin around on nobody. You remember what happened last year, don't you?"

Martin was annoyed that Charlie would bring that up. He rolled his eyes and said, "Of course I do! How could I forget? And that's exactly why I'm worried right now!"

"Well, if you're gonna be mad at somebody, you need to be mad at yourself. If you'da been here when you said you would, none of—"

Martin held up his hand to silence him. "I know! Now be quiet for a minute while I try to think about what we need to do!"

"What do you mean, you need to think about what we need to do? There's only one thing for us *to do*," said Charlie. "Let's go find him. He can't have gotten too far. Maybe he's still around the plaza somewhere. And if not, maybe someone there has seen him."

Martin nodded in agreement. "Fine. We were supposed to meet each other down at the northeastern entrance. Maybe he's just hangin around down there. I know he wanted us to ask around about a . . ." He tapped his foot as he tried to recall the name. "Alonso Cordova—nickname's Poncho."

"Alright then. Let's head down to the plaza right now and ask around about this Mr. Cordova."

The two of them began to walk down the ramp towards the docks. "This should be interestin," said Martin. "Neither of us is really all that great with Spanish."

"Oh really?" Charlie laughed down the ramp at Martin. "You sure didn't have any problem talkin to that little lady and gettin her to take you home last night."

Martin rolled his eyes as he made it down to the dock. "We really didn't talk all that much."

Charlie made it to the dock as well. "How were you plannin to help him out if y'all went down to the plaza to ask around for this Mr. Cordova?"

"I don't know. This is a port town. I reckon we figured there ought to be somebody down there who can speak English and Spanish. We could get them to help us."

"Fine," said Charlie, "let's do that then."

The two went to the plaza and asked around with Martin's limited Spanish, but after an hour of searching they had no success.

Finally, Charlie said, "Listen, it's a waste of time tryin to find him this way. I think we need to just go on and tell my brother what's happened."

"Let's look a little while longer," Martin said.

Charlie reluctantly agreed.

For the next hour they continued asking around in and near the plaza, but they still had no luck. They were pretty sure that a few of the people they approached did speak English and

Spanish, but they must not have wanted to get involved in whatever Martin and Charlie were up to.

"Maybe he's already gone back to the *Gypsy*," Charlie offered.

"Maybe so," agreed Martin.

They went back to the sloop, but no one had seen Adam.

Captain Phillips knew his little brother. He could tell right away something was amiss by the way Charlie and Martin were acting.

"What's the problem, boys?" he asked.

Charlie and Martin exchanged worried glances, and then Charlie began to explain, "We've been lookin for Fletcher. He and Smith here were supposed to go lookin for that man this mornin, but he was late gettin there, so Adam took off without him. Now we don't know where he's gone or when he'll be back."

"We've been lookin for him for the last two hours," said Martin.

"You *were* supposed to go with him, Smith. I know you were, because I heard y'all talkin about it myself when we were leavin the tavern last night." The captain closed his eyes and pressed his fingers against the bridge of his nose before he looked up at Martin and said, "Why weren't you here this mornin when you said you'd be?"

Martin took a deep breath and shrugged his shoulders before responding. "Can't really say, Cap'n. I guess I lost track of the time."

"Mm-hm." The captain narrowed his eyes at Martin, but all he said was, "Where all were you two were plannin to go to look for that fella?"

Charlie intervened. "They were just goin to go ask around

down in the Plaza Vieja to see if they could find anybody who might know the man."

The captain nodded. "Hmph. Well, daylight's burnin, boys, and it'll be nighttime before we know it. I reckon y'all better try and get some local help so you can track him down."

"Local help? Do you know anybody here?" asked Charlie.

The captain lowered his head and thought for a moment. He disappeared into his quarters and came back out with a slip of paper. "Here, take this."

He handed the paper to his brother.

Charlie looked at it. "It's a name and address."

The captain nodded. "Yep. Another one of Emmanuel's friends. He's a local fellow. I've never met him, though. Got one of them long names . . ." He strained to read the writing, then said it aloud: "Santiago Velasquez de Leon. He's captain of *La Dama del Caribe*."

Martin's eyes got big. "Captain Velasquez? Of course! I know him! We did business with his ship just last year—right after Adam joined the company as a matter of fact."

"Good," said Charlie. "Let's go then."

"Hopefully, y'all will be able to track down this captain and then find the boy. And if you go to that address and the captain ain't around, I'm sure they can find somebody else who can help you."

Charlie and Martin wasted no time getting back to the dock and running into town to look for the address on the piece of paper.

Chapter Five

As Adam rode along with the two men in the horse cart, he learned the man with the green eyes was called Carlos. They headed west down the main road away from the city center. Hector asked Adam, "You say you was coming with ship from America, yes?"

"Mm-hm. The ship is called the *Carolina Gypsy*. We're supposed to be leaving first thing in the morning to head back home."

"I see. Then it is very important that you finding this Señor Cordova today."

Adam nodded. "That's right. Speaking of which, how much longer should it be until we get to the house of this Cordova family?" He looked at his watch and then put it back into his pocket.

Hector spoke to Carlos, and of course Adam had no clue

what they were saying other than he did hear the name Cordova mentioned.

Carlos shrugged and gave what looked like a defensive response. Adam hated that he couldn't understand the conversation.

Hector turned his attention back to Adam. "It not being too much longer now."

"What were you two talking about?"

"Ah, I just telling Carlos that we needing to hurry to go to the house of Cordova, and you needing to go away in the morning *bien temprano*—very early, yes?"

Adam nodded. As they rode along, he began to suspect that they weren't taking him to see any Cordova family, but then he told himself he was probably worrying too much because of what had happened to him the year before. He tried to relax and enjoy the view of the countryside.

At one point they crossed a narrow little stream. Adam wondered if it was part of a bigger river or just a creek. All he knew was that they were a good distance out of the city now.

When he looked at his pocket watch, he saw that it had already been close to an hour since they had left the market. He would think they should be at the house of this family soon if it was two hours away walking, but there didn't seem to be any houses in sight, and in fact it seemed like they were headed towards some kind of dense forest.

After debating whether or not he should ask Hector about where they were, he finally decided to do it. "Are we lost?"

Hector looked at Carlos, then back at Adam. "Why you saying that, señor?"

"We're headed into that forest. Unless this Cordova family

lives in some kind of hovel in those woods up ahead, then I can't imagine we're on our way to any house."

"This forest—this is only a little one. We going through to the other side right now."

At that moment Adam knew he was being lied to. He also knew that since he was in the middle of nowhere with these men, he had to be smart and calculate a plan rather than just trying to hop out of the cart.

"You know, fellas, I think I might as well have you take me back to town. I mean, I'll still pay you and all, but I'm afraid if we keep going I won't make it back to the ship on time tonight, and that would get me into all kinds of trouble."

"If you waiting a little more, we being there soon," said a grinning Hector.

Adam shook his head. "Nah. You know, let's just turn around and head on back to town. I reckon I've changed my mind about trying to find this Señor Cordova, anyway."

This time Hector didn't respond to Adam, but to Carlos he said, "¡*Apurate*!" Then it sounded to Adam like he issued some sort of command.

Carlos snapped the reins, and the horse sped up.

The only thing Adam kept thinking was, *Oh Lord, not again. Please don't let these two dump me in the middle of nowhere out here.*

Fortunately, once they had ventured well into the dense forest, Carlos stopped the horse cart, and he and Hector turned around to face Adam.

"What is this?" Adam asked.

"Listen, amigo," Hector began, "we no having no plans to harm you, but we do needing to borrow you for a little while."

"What are you talking about?"

"Very soon we arriving to a place—a safe place for you if you are behaving yourself. And all you having to do is sit quiet for a day or two."

"What?! My crew is supposed to be leaving Havana tomorrow, and I have to be on that ship."

Carlos made some extended observation to Hector, then appeared to suggest something to his associate.

Hector shook his head. "*No es necesario.* That will not be necessary, right, amigo?" he asked Adam.

Knowing he couldn't understand what Carlos had said, Hector decided to translate. "He say we should tying you up so you cannot be escaping."

Adam would not react.

"I not thinking we need to worrying about you, amigo," said Hector. "You is not thinking of escaping, yes?"

Adam's face was like steel. He refused to let these men see what he was feeling. He swore to himself the previous year after he had survived another dangerous set of circumstances that he'd never again show fear to another man, or beg another man for his life. He hated the way he felt that day he had begged Ajax and Lot to not leave him on that island. He knew the only thing that ultimately saved him was Providence. Emmanuel had had many conversations with him about that very thing after he was rescued, and Adam came to realize that his life would go on up until the time God had appointed for him to die—and it would not happen one moment sooner or later.

"You listen good to me," said Hector. "Listen very good. Carlos, he taking a message back to your *barco*—your ship—that we is holding you in a secret place, and if they wanting you back they have to give us whatever we telling them."

"You must be joking!" Adam laughed hard. "You actually

think that you're going to send a message back to our American ship that you are demanding ransom—for me? This was my first time on that ship. I have no skills for them. They won't pay tuppence for me, you idiot."

In reality, Adam knew his shipmates on the *Gypsy* would do whatever might be necessary to try to help any of the men on board that ship if they found themselves in trouble, but he wasn't about to comfort these two rogues with that kind of knowledge.

Hector looked at Carlos, annoyed, then took a deep breath before he said to Adam. "*Ya veremos.* We will see."

Chapter Six

MARTIN AND CHARLIE had walked up and down San Pedro Street along the waterfront a dozen times looking for a house or apartment with the name Velasquez, but to no avail.

Most of the little houses that lined the road were marked with names outside like Ramirez, Martinez, Garcia, Rosado, and so forth, but they'd not seen anything that even looked close to Velasquez. Finally, Charlie said, "This is a waste of time. Why don't we just ask someone? This might not even be the right street. Maybe it's not San Pedro, but San . . . Paul or somethin."

"Fine," said Martin.

He marched across the street and asked a man who appeared to be a guard occupying a watch house near what looked like some kind of estate. In slow and halting Spanish, with a Carolina accent, he said, "Ah, *perdon, señor. Yo necesito hablar . . . ah . . . un hombre.* Ah . . . *el Capitán Santiago Velasquez de Leon. ¿Ayuda?"*

He showed the man the piece of paper with the captain's name and the street on which he lived, and waited for an answer.

Although Martin's Spanish left a lot to be desired, Charlie was impressed. It was more exotic words than he could string together in any language.

The guard looked at the paper, then studied the young men. He gave a lengthy response in Spanish that sounded like it ended with a question. Martin didn't understand much of it, but he did understand something about the captain living nearby.

"What'd he say?" asked Charlie.

Martin barely shook his head, not wanting to appear too obvious, but he responded, "I'm not sure. I think he wants to know how we know the captain."

"Well, answer him."

Martin cleared his throat. "Ah . . . *El capitán* . . . ah . . . *es un amigo de* . . . ah . . . *mi* . . . Oh Lord, how do you say 'boss'? Ah . . . *patrón?"*

"*¿Quien es su patrón, señor?"* the guard asked.

"*Mi patrón se llama Emmanuel Rogers. Somos de North Carolina en America."*

The guard scratched his head, seemingly unsure of what to do. He made a motion to indicate that he wanted the men to wait while he went to the main house.

Martin stood there, impatiently waiting for the guard to return.

"What were y'all sayin?" asked Charlie.

"I told him who we were lookin for. I think he said the Velasquez house is near here. He wanted to know if we knew the captain. I told him we did—that he was a friend of our boss.

Then he wanted to know who our boss was, so I told him. And I told him where we were from."

"So what's he gone inside for?" asked Charlie.

Martin shrugged.

They saw the guard start making his way back down the lane towards the gate and open it.

"*Ven conmigo*," said the guard, motioning for them to follow him.

Martin gave a friendly slap to Charlie's shoulder and then ran ahead to follow the guard. They went into a courtyard, then across a terrace, at which point the guard turned them over to a black servant, who worked in the enormous house on the estate. He wore a white blouse and white trousers, as they soon noticed did all of the servants on the property.

"*Siganme, por favor*," said the servant.

He started to walk into the house, but Martin and Charlie weren't following him. He looked back and motioned for them to come along, so they scurried to catch up. They had noticed that the several workers out on the grounds and those who were serving in the house all appeared to be African slaves, although neither Martin nor Charlie had ever seen so many slaves belonging to one family. For that matter they had never seen slaves speaking Spanish. Still, they realized it was entirely logical that they would speak the same language as their masters.

The ornate columns and blue mosaic tiles in the house were impressive. The floors looked like they were made of marble, and the domed ceilings were exquisitely painted. The chandeliers and sconces dripped with crystal, and the furniture was intricately carved and upholstered in plush velvets and patterned silks. The luxury of the place took their breath away. There were no houses like this back home. Not even close. Beaufort's wealthiest citizens had impressive homes, no doubt, but this could nearly be called a palace.

For a moment Martin and Charlie had nearly forgotten they were there to try to find Captain Velasquez. As enjoyable as it was touring what was clearly one of Havana's finest homes, they had a friend and shipmate to track down. They were hoping someone would show up soon to tell them where they needed to go.

The servant finally led them into what appeared to be a grand office and library. Martin was stunned when he recognized the man sitting behind the desk as Captain Velásquez himself.

"¡*Bienvenidos, chicos*!" said the handsome young captain as he stood and walked around his desk to greet them.

"Captain Velasquez!" said Martin. "I never expected to find you here."

"Why not?" asked the captain, laughing. "This is my house."

"Well, this place is . . ." Martin looked around the room, unable to find the words to convey his utter shock.

"You did not expect a—how you say?—'old salt' to be living in a place like this?"

Martin and Charlie both shook their heads in disbelief.

"To tell you the truth, this house was built by my father's family, *que Dios le bendiga*." He bowed his head and crossed himself. "He is dead now, but my mother is living still, *gracias a Dios*. My heart is on my ship, *La Dama del Caribe*, but when I am here in Havana I stay with her so she will not be alone."

"Well, it's really . . . extraordinary," said Martin, looking around the room. "Really. I don't even know what to say."

"I thank you," said the captain. "So tell me: What brings you here today?"

"Right, well, our ship—Emmanuel Rogers's ship, the *Carolina Gypsy*—is supposed to leave tomorrow, but one of the members of our crew—he's Emmanuel's apprentice—took off on his own this mornin, and we need to find him and make sure he's back on board by nightfall."

"What is this having to do with me?" said the captain.

"We've been lookin all over town for him, but my Spanish isn't so good, and so far we've had no luck. Emmanuel told us if we ran into any troubles here in Havana, that we should come to you—that you're a friend of his."

The captain nodded his head in understanding. "I see, but how can I help? I don't know this boy. I am not knowing where he has gone. Did he tell any of you any pieces of information?"

Charlie spoke up. "Yes. Martin here was supposed to meet him this mornin to go looking for a man, but Martin got there late, and Adam was already gone."

"Would you stop blamin me?" said Martin. "That's the second time you—"

The captain interrupted before the boys could start arguing. "Maybe this young man don't want to go tomorrow on the ship." He grinned and held out his arms as he motioned around. "Maybe he likes it here in beautiful Havana."

"You don't understand," said Martin. "Emmanuel will kill us if we don't get this boy back to North Carolina."

"Not to mention his mother," said Charlie.

"So this is a young boy?" asked the captain.

"He's barely eighteen," said Martin. "He's Emmanuel's apprentice, and this was his first trip to the Caribbean. Emmanuel told us if we don't come back with the boy, we might as well not come back at all."

The captain shook his head. "Emmanuel Rogers is a

friend for a very long time. This boy must mean a great deal to him if he say that to you."

"Aw, well if you know Emmanuel," said Martin, "then you know his company is the only family he's got."

The captain nodded. "I understand." He thought for a moment, then said, "All right, I help you, but I need to know what information you have. Havana is much bigger than your little town, so your friend could be anywhere. Let us just hope he has not left the main town."

"Thank you, Captain Velásquez!" said Martin.

"Yes, thank you," said Charlie.

"Please, call me Santiago. When we're on *La Dama*, call me *capitán*, but here Santiago is fine."

"Alright, Santiago," said Martin. "Well, as we were sayin, I was supposed to meet Adam this mornin at the northeastern gate of the Plaza Vieja. He had been given a name of someone he was lookin for, so maybe he's found him. Thing is, we don't know the man, so we wouldn't know where to check."

"What is the name of the man?" said Santiago. "I live my whole life here. I know many people, so maybe we can find who this is."

"The man's name is Alonso Cordova. His nickname is Poncho."

Santiago looked pensive. "Alonso Cordova? Hmm . . . And why was this boy looking for this Alonso Cordova? What did he want with him?"

Martin and Charlie looked at each other. They appeared to be trying to decide whether or not to tell him what they knew.

"Listen, boys," Santiago told them. "I will be happy to offer you my help, but you need to tell me what you know. Otherwise, we may miss something that is important."

Martin said, "Adam heard from his grandfather—well, he's like his grandfather—that Poncho Cordova might know something about his father. Apparently, his father left Beaufort before he was born, and this Poncho was a friend of his."

Santiago wrinkled his brow. "Why would this old man not just tell him the father's name? Would that not be much easier for him to find information?"

"Of course it would," said Martin, "except Adam's mother made Valentine—that's the old man—promise that he would not tell Adam anything about his father. But she never made him promise not to tell anything about people who might have known his father."

Santiago chuckled. "I see. Well, that is clever of the old man."

"So do you know this man? This Alonso Cordova?" asked Martin.

"I knew of him."

"What does that mean?" asked Charlie.

"Well, if he is the man I am thinking of, he is dead."

"What?" asked Martin. "Are you sure? When did this happen?"

"Yes, I am sure," said Santiago. "I think it was about ten years ago."

"Then where's Adam?" Charlie wondered aloud.

Martin looked at him, his brain still a little slow from the headache. "Huh?"

"I mean, if he already found out that fellow died, he ought to have gone on back to the *Gypsy*. He's been gone hours now."

"Maybe it's another Alonso Cordova," offered Martin. "Is that possible?" He looked at Santiago for some response.

Santiago gave a halting nod. "It is possible, but it is not the most common name. What do you know about this Alonso Cordova—the one this boy looks for?"

"Only that he was a sailor. Valentine said he sailed with Adam's father and that they were close friends."

Santiago clicked his tongue and shook his head sorrowfully. "Hmm . . . There are many sailors in Havana, and I suppose it is possible that there could be more than one, but I'm afraid this was probably the same man. The Alonso Cordova that I knew was also a sailor—at least he was at one time."

"Then you must know some people who knew him," said Martin. "Maybe Adam has found his family or somethin and gone to see them."

"You say that you think he went into La Plaza Vieja, looking for this man?"

Martin and Charlie both nodded.

"This is the problem, boys. There are many—how you say it?—bandits who work down in the plaza. They wait for men from out of town to show up looking for help and then they will trick them and rob them, or sometimes even kidnap them for ransom."

"See!" Martin exclaimed to Charlie. "This is exactly why I was worried. These kinds of things happen! And Adam would just have to be the one that these kinds of things happen to on this trip."

"You ought not assume the worst, Martin," Charlie argued. "He might even be back at the *Gypsy* already."

"You said that same thing over an hour ago," countered Martin.

Santiago shook his head, visibly annoyed at Martin and

Charlie's arguing. "Boys, this is not helpful. Let me just get my things, and we will go and look for your friend."

"Fine," said Charlie.

"Fine," Martin agreed.

Chapter Seven

ADAM AND HIS captors continued traveling a little farther into the forest with the horse cart until the cleared path came to an end. At that point Carlos and Hector untied the horse from the cart and began to march Adam deeper into the woods on foot. Carlos walked in front and led the horse. Hector stayed behind Adam. Both men wore machetes on their belts, but now Hector had his in his right hand to ensure that Adam kept moving as instructed. In his left hand Hector held a palm branch, which he swept back and forth behind him every so often to make sure their footmarks were covered over with foliage.

It would've seemed to make more sense if at least one of the men were riding the horse, but the vegetation was so thick in places—intentionally, or so it seemed—that Carlos often had to bend back branches just so they could pass through. Adam figured they did it that way to keep the path mostly hidden. He certainly had no idea in which direction they would go once they stopped the cart. Everything looked wild and overgrown.

They walked. And walked. And walked some more. It was damp and sticky and hot. At one point the horse reared up. Quicker than Adam realized what was happening, Carlos swung his machete forward and chopped off the head of an enormous snake.

Oh Lord, thought Adam, *that thing's even bigger than the cottonmouths back home!*

"Do not worry," said Hector. "This serpent, she not having poison. She just crushing you to death." He squeezed both hands in front of him as if he were wringing out a wet cloth.

As they walked by the body of the serpent, still wriggling on the ground, Hector picked it up and tossed it across the forest. Then he stabbed the head with his machete and flung it as well.

"Why'd you do that?" said Adam.

"Why not?" said Hector. "Think about it! That serpent did not just having his head fall off. Leaving her here might giving away our path. We not wanting to give away our path."

It was frustrating. Adam thought about how he could leave some clues along the way, but with Hector following so close behind him, he didn't have a chance to do anything of the sort.

After about another twenty minutes of walking, they were no longer having to spread vegetation to make their way down the path but rather were on a well-cleared walkway. They were so deep in the forest at this point, though, that it no longer mattered whether or not anyone could see their trail. In the distance Adam saw several grass-thatched roofs begin to appear. As they got closer, he could could tell that it was a camp of sorts.

There were two crudely constructed buildings—a long, rectangular one and a short, square one. Then there was a third building that looked like it was higher quality—at least as much as could be said for a hut in the middle of a tropical forest.

Considering all of the dense vegetation, it appeared to be a fortress for some kind of militia—maybe an abandoned one. While there weren't many men out in the open, the ones who were looked like a motley bunch.

"What is this place?" Adam inquired.

Hector and Carlos laughed.

"*Ay*, amigo, this is our business," said Hector. "We not having a lot of customers, but it is—how you saying?—very . . . ah . . . *lucrativo*."

"And illegal," Adam remarked. "So your business is kidnapping foreigners for money."

"That is my business today, yes, but we doing many kinds of things, because we having many different skills. Every man here is having his own job to do. On this day my job is bringing you here."

Adam raised his eyebrows, surprised at the answer.

Just then Carlos excused himself from the conversation and walked the horse towards what looked like a horse pen and stable. Hector seemed to shout out some instructions to him very quickly in Spanish, to which Carlos waved dismissively and continued walking.

"Look there," Hector said to Adam, pointing to a small, skinny man with a very long, thin moustache that drooped around the two sides of his mouth. "He is Flaco. His skill is as a *ladrón*. He is the king of *los ladrones*."

Adam gave him a confused look. "*Ladrón?*"

Hector flipped out his hand and said matter-of-factly, "He

is a thief. He is the best thief. Real fast, real quiet." He pointed to another man, heavyset, balding, and probably in his forties. "See him? He is *un asesino*. Do you know what *asesino* is?"

Adam shook his head. "I don't know. Asinine?"

"It means assassin. He is being very good at killing a man with his hands only, very fast."

Adam had no idea exactly what that was supposed to mean, and he didn't really care. He knew he wouldn't be hanging around long enough to get to know everybody. All he was interested in was figuring out how many men were posted at this hideout and where they all were.

"Do you live here?" he asked Hector. "I mean, you do all your mischief back in the city and then crawl back into the forest to sleep?"

"Yes," said Hector as if it were the most normal thing in the world.

"How many of you are there?"

Hector smiled. He led Adam into the smallest of the three buildings, a crudely built but apparently strong hut that he soon learned was a prison of sorts. There was another man being held inside, chained to the wall.

"There are enough of us to making sure you not going anywhere," said Hector.

Adam wrinkled his eyebrows and must've looked concerned, because Hector added, "Do not worry—I not tying you up if you not trying anything stupid. But you trying anything stupid, and you be in chain like that one, or worse." He grabbed at his own neck and made a squeezing motion, simulating being choked to death, and Adam quickly understood his meaning.

"You having any weapons?" Hector asked.

Adam thought about his pocketknife, which he kept in

his boot. "See for yourself," he said, then held out his arms and stood up straight, inviting Hector to search him.

Hector patted him down along his arms and torso and legs but seemed to be satisfied to find the boy had only a pocket watch and some money.

"I taking these right now," he said, grabbing the two items and putting them into his own pocket.

"Take the money, but how about if you let me keep the pocket watch?" said Adam. "It was a gift."

Hector laughed. "Yes? And now you giving it to me."

Adam rolled his eyes and chuckled. "Alright. You go right ahead." He looked at him calmly and said, "I can promise you, though—I will get it back."

"Sure, *compadre*," said Hector, chuckling. He patted Adam on the shoulder and then left the prison hut and locked the door.

Chapter Eight

SINCE THE PLAZA was near the harbor, Santiago suggested to Martin and Charlie that they first go back to the *Gypsy* once more to see if anyone had heard any news about Adam— or maybe he had returned. Unfortunately, there was no word of him.

They went straight from there to the plaza, and Santiago took Martin and Charlie to the first place he thought of for getting information—and it happened to be the *fonda* where Adam had eaten earlier that day. The workers said they had many Americans dining there that morning, but they weren't sure if the boy they were looking for had been among them.

Next the captain led them to a couple of the vendors with the largest stalls full of wares—they tended to attract visitors. Again, no luck.

Finally, Santiago spotted a peanut vendor enter the plaza.

"*Gracias a Dios!*" he said. "I know this man. I was looking for him earlier, but he was not here," he explained to Martin and Charlie.

Immediately, he strode over to him, with the young men in tow, and began to speak very rapidly in Spanish. Martin and Charlie were completely lost as to what they were saying. Eventually, the peanut vendor motioned towards the northwest gate of the plaza, and they began to think he may have helpful information.

Santiago then explained to the boys what the man had said. "He thinks the boy you are looking for was here earlier this morning, trying to ask around about something, but he could not understand what he wanted to know, since he does not speak English."

"That's great news! Did he say where he went?" asked Martin.

The captain took a deep breath. "It is not so great news. This could be very bad. He says that he saw the boy go with a man who is one of these bandits like I mentioned to you."

"What? Where would they have gone?" asked Charlie.

"This I do not know," said Santiago. He thanked the peanut vendor so he could go back to making money, then said to the young men, "He said he saw them leave through the northwest gate there, but that does not tell us much. It goes in many directions beyond that point, so we cannot know where they went. All we can do is start searching and hope we find something that will help us. If we have no luck, then we will put up a reward for information about the boy."

"When you say he was a bandit," said Martin, "what kind of bandit is he? I just don't understand why Adam would've gone off with somebody like that."

"What was the boy doing here this morning? You say he was looking for this Alonso Cordova? How? Does he even speak Spanish?"

Martin and Charlie both shook their heads.

"Then he was needing to find someone who speaks English," Santiago observed. "This man might be one who preys on foreigners. It is impossible to say where they might have gone, but the sooner we start looking for them, the better."

They left back out through the southeast gate. Their horses were tied up near there. Santiago paid the man who was watching them, and they all mounted up and were about to leave when they heard one of the crew members of the *Gypsy* calling out to them, out of breath.

It was Jones. "I've been all over the place searchin for you lot. Look at this!"

He handed Martin something that looked like a note. The wax seal had been broken, so it had obviously been already read by Jones and whoever else was on the *Gypsy* when it arrived.

Martin tried to read it aloud. He strained at the penmanship, but he was able to make out at least the start of it. "'We having you friend. He is safe for now, but if you wanting him back, deliver twelve hundred pesos or'—what does this say?" He showed the letter to Santiago.

"It says *dos veces*—two times that in *bienes de calidad*— quality goods to the place on this marked map by tomorrow morning before *amanecer*—daybreak. After that time, within six hours we will . . ." He struggled to read what was next in the letter. "*¡Ay! ¡Que un palurdo!* This man writes like a child! I think it says they will be delivering him somewhere near the plaza by noon. At the bottom it says if we do not meet their demands, they will kill him and only deliver his head."

"Twelve hundred pesos. How many pounds is that?" asked Martin.

"I think it is about four pesos to a pound, so that would be three hundred pounds," answered Santiago.

"Good Lord!" exclaimed Charlie. "We don't have that kind of money lyin around! We'd have to go into the revenue from the cargo."

"I would think that was the purpose of this little exercise," said Santiago. "Men like these, they know cargo ships are on strict schedules, so they do not worry much about the authorities getting involved. They do not demand an enormous ransom, but it is still quite a lot. Enough to make them a handsome profit, but not so much that many are unwilling to pay it just so they can be on their way."

"What choice do we have, then?" asked Charlie. "Let's go back and talk to my brother and arrange the payment. We obviously can't go back without Adam. Even if Emmanuel doesn't kill us, Mary Fletcher will."

"No, you idiot," said Martin dismissively. "We can't just deliver the money. We have no guarantee that they'll even return Adam like they say. They're criminals. It's not like we can trust 'em!"

Santiago nodded. "Your friend is right. We need to go back to the ship and get a few more men. Then we will make a plan. We will get your friend back, but that is not all. We are going to put a stop to these criminals. They are a pestilence in Havana, and I am going to see to it that they are brought to justice."

Chapter Nine

As SOON AS Hector had locked him in the prison hut, Adam tried to push on the door to try to figure out how it was locked, since he hadn't noticed while he was being thrown inside. A gun was fired just outside the hut, and Hector shouted as he banged on the door and warned Adam, "I said to you nothing stupid. I was not joking with you, *chico*."

Adam backed away from the door. He wouldn't try that again. Anyway, he had found out what he wanted to know. By the way that the door gave a little bit but then held tight on one side, he figured there must be a padlock of some sort securing the entry.

He turned to the man who was chained to the wall and said, "You speak English?"

The prisoner, who looked gaunt and emaciated, shrugged. He apparently didn't understand.

Adam walked along the perimeter of the room to see how well the hut was constructed. The log walls were full of gaps, but they were very strong, and they extended a good ways down into the ground. It occurred to him that even if he could come up with a way out of that prison, it'd be a huge risk, since he was in the middle of a dense forest and at this point had no idea how to get back to the city.

He needed time to think—and to pray for a miracle.

Not long after sunset Adam began to hear the sound of huge waves crashing against the shore. *That means we're near the ocean*, he thought. He hadn't realized that before, since the men had led him so far out of town and deep into the woods, but apparently they had wended their way in a more northerly direction as they were traveling. It had been hard to keep track of which way they were going, because the sun was so obscured by the trees. But then maybe that had been the whole point.

The floor was covered by woven grass mats. Adam wondered what the ground was like underneath them. *I'm going to dig out of this thing*, he thought. *If I can make it to the ocean, I can find my way back to town.*

He peeled back one of the mats closest to the wall and scraped at the damp, sandy ground with his hands. As he tried to dig, his mind started running fast. Little worries began nagging at him. *This is almost too easy. They have to know I can dig right out of here. There could be somebody waiting to kill me as soon as I crawl out the other side.*

In the end Adam didn't care, though. He was doubtful of his captors' ability to find the *Gypsy* to demand their ransom. In fact, he didn't even know what kind of payment they were demanding even if they did find the ship, or if Captain Phillips would have that kind of money on board. Regardless, he wasn't going to risk sticking around to find out what would happen if the transaction didn't go through as planned. The last thing he wanted would be to end up chained to the wall like that other man—or worse, as Hector had threatened.

He started digging faster. When he came to some roots, he remembered the pocketknife he had in his boot. He pulled it out and cut at the roots, then used it to break up the ground. Before long he had a decent hole made, but he knew he'd need to do something with the dirt he'd displaced.

He lifted the floor mats to each side of the one he had been digging beneath and began to spread out the mound of dirt under them.

All of a sudden the man chained to the wall said, "*¡Oye, tu!*"

Adam turned to look at him. "What?"

"*¡Idiota! ¿No piensas que yo ya habia tratado esa misma cosa?*"

Adam just shrugged. "I have no idea what you're saying, man. I'm sorry."

The man pointed with his free arm to one of the mats on the floor near where he was chained to the wall.

"What is it?" said Adam.

He shouted something, then made a come-here motion to Adam and pointed angrily at the mat beside him. Adam covered the hole he was digging with a mat, then went over and lifted the mat the man was pointing at. There was evidence of a huge hole underneath that had been filled back in. Once the man was satisfied that Adam had seen the hole, he motioned to the chain that had him fastened to the wall. "*¡Esto es lo que te pasará si te encuentran cavando!*"

"Hmm." Adam took stock of the situation. He figured

out what the man was saying, or at least he got the gist. "Well, I'm not going to just sit here," he told the man. "They'd probably chain me up anyway. Then I'll be as bad off as you. Sorry, fella. I've at least got to try to get out of this place."

The man stared at him blankly, then rolled his eyes.

Adam returned to the place where he had been digging and went back to work. Suddenly, he heard the lock rattle outside the door. He covered over the hole with the mat, then went over to a different wall, sat down, and rested his head on his arms, which were crossed on top of his knees as though he had been napping.

He popped his head up just long enough to motion "Shh!" to the other man, then put his head back down. Seconds later another man—one Adam hadn't seen before—came through the door, tore half a loaf of bread into two pieces, and threw one piece at each of the prisoners.

"You got anything to wash this down with?" Adam asked sarcastically, knowing full well the man probably didn't even understand what he was saying.

The man narrowed his eyes at him and then went back out and locked the door again.

Adam looked over at the other prisoner. "Now I see why you're so skinny." He got up from where he was sitting and gave his piece of bread to him. "Looks like you need it more than I do, fella. I'm getting out of here tonight."

The prisoner looked surprised. He nodded his head and said, "*Gracias. Que Dios te bendiga.*"

Adam understood the *gracias* part, so he said, "You're welcome."

He continued digging, then spreading out the displaced dirt. He noticed the man reach into a bucket that was beside him with his hand and drink. He realized that it was a water bucket and not what he had previously assumed it to be. That made him wonder what the man did use as a privy. Then he decided it'd be better if he didn't think too hard trying to figure that one out.

Every so often he'd creep around inside the building and peer through the cracks in the walls to see if he could determine what was happening outside. While there were a few lamps lit around the fortress, he didn't see anyone out there. He was able to hear noise coming from the large building on the other side of the hut. He was guessing that must be some kind of common room. It sounded like there were a lot of men. Far more than he had noticed around the grounds earlier in the day.

Once he had dug down deep enough on his side of the wall so that he felt sure he'd be able to fit through, he decided to stop digging until everything was quiet in the camp. He knew he wouldn't make a run for it while men were still awake and wandering around outside.

He decided to stop and rest awhile, and since his hands weren't busy, his thoughts drifted back home . . . He wished he could be back at the Topsail Tavern. It was around this same time last year that Adam had left his home at the tavern to go work for Emmanuel, and now he wondered if he'd make it back.

He thought about his poor mother, and he was glad she had no way of knowing his circumstances right now. She nearly fell apart when he disappeared last year. He briefly contemplated how she'd handle it if the *Gypsy* arrived back in Beaufort and he wasn't on it. It was an awful thought that he quickly pushed out of his mind. Plain and simple, he knew she'd never get over it. She never wanted him to go on that trip in the first place. In fact, she had burst into tears the day he told her that he was going.

Then he started thinking about Laney Martin. *I'm gonna*

marry that girl eventually, he thought. He remembered the day he first went up and introduced himself to her at Rasquelle's party. He didn't think he'd actually have a chance with her, but he didn't care. He had spotted the honey-blond, green-eyed beauty from across the lawn and knew he had to at least talk to her. It took his disappearance last year to get her to finally warm up to him. Since that time the two had become close friends—well, as much as any young man and young woman could be without tongues wagging relentlessly. He remembered how happy she was when she learned he had been rescued, and when she found out what he had uncovered, she actually called him her hero. Just knowing that she thought of him in that way made Adam feel confident— not that he ever needed help in that area. Thinking about her set his heart racing again, but right now he needed to focus on his current circumstances. It was time to get out of that hut and on his way back to the ship.

How cruel it would be if he never made it back to Beaufort. It wasn't an option that he was willing to consider. He was about to check his pocket watch when he remembered that Hector had taken it from him. *Eh . . . what difference does it make what time it is?* he thought. He would just wait to start digging again when everything was quiet outside and he was sure that everyone—or most everyone—was asleep.

Chapter Ten

SANTIAGO, MARTIN, AND Charlie ended up making one detour before they went back to the *Gypsy* to formulate a plan. Santiago had an English friend who had been living in Havana since even before the British took temporary control of the city in 1762.

Thomas Drake—apparently no relation to Sir Francis Drake, at least none that he would claim—had come to Cuba many years earlier and fallen in love with the place, so he decided to settle down there.

Drake was an intrepid adventurer who loved a challenge. In fact, he thrived on adversity. Santiago was sure that bringing him into the fold as they came up with a plan to not only rescue Adam but to put a stop to these criminals would be beneficial.

The four men—Santiago, Drake, Martin, and Charlie—explained their ideas to Captain Phillips and the crew as soon as they boarded the *Gypsy*. The plan, at its core, would involve getting money together and then leaving it as the requested ransom, but only as a decoy. While the ransom would be a lot for the crew of the *Gypsy* to come up with, it was something Santiago could easily provide as a favor to his old friend Emmanuel. Not just that, but he explained he was absolutely determined to follow that money to its destination and to recover it, along with Emmanuel's apprentice. It was a relief to Captain Phillips, since having to dip into the ship's coffers could be catastrophic if they had to return with both the money and the boy gone.

There would need to be someone to wait back on the ship in case Adam returned, but that would be easy, since the captain was already planning to stick around to work on rigging repairs. Another contingent would go to the location where the ransom was to be left and lie in wait until someone else brought the ransom and left it in the designated location. That man would then leave, and those in hiding nearby would continue to wait until they saw someone come to pick up the money. Once the ransom was collected, they would follow whoever it was at a distance until they arrived at their intended destination—presumably the bandits' hideout.

Meanwhile, back in town, friends of Santiago and Drake, with the help of the peanut vendor who had seen Adam following Hector out of the plaza, would be covertly waiting around all four entrances to the market square so that if and when Adam was released, they could apprehend the men who brought him into town and try to extract information from them about their operation.

Since the letter said Adam wouldn't be released near the plaza until noon—a full six hours after the money was to be delivered—their hope was to make it to the bandits' hideout, taking them by surprise, and rescue Adam, then apprehend anyone involved with the scheme and bring them bound and tied back into Havana to be handed over to the local authorities.

It was decided that Santiago, Drake, Martin, and Charlie, along with Jones, Willis, and Canady, would be the ones to hide near the location indicated for the ransom.

Santiago enlisted one of his most trusted servants from his family's estate to deliver the ransom, which was to be made at a little building—although they couldn't tell from the map whether it was supposed to be a hut or an old guard house—near the ruins of the Torreon de la Chorrera, a fortified tower that had been blasted by British cannons during the siege of Havana a few years earlier.

Once their plan had been formulated and thoroughly discussed, the only thing left to do was wait.

As the core group of men sat around outside the tower looking out onto the Atlantic, some of them shared stories about their own previous encounters with rogues and scoundrels.

Santiago explained that he had only ever had to kill men on one occasion, close to a decade earlier when he was sailing between the Philippines and Malaysia and a crazed group of Iranun pirates tried to overtake his vessel. He and his crew fought bravely and ultimately defeated the ruffians, sending them sinking to the depths of the Sulu Sea. He said he didn't relish taking a man's life, but he was not about to let thieves snatch his livelihood from him by force.

The group numbers dwindled as men wandered off to the makeshift pallets they had made inside the ruins of the tower. Eventually, Martin was the only *Gypsy* crew member out there with Drake and Santiago. All three of them were feeling too anxious to sleep.

Drake asked Martin, "How long have you and this Fletcher boy been friends?"

Martin drank a sip of whisky from the flask he had brought before he began to explain. "Believe it or not, I only met Adam last year."

Drake looked surprised. "Is that so? You seem to think very much of him, like you have known him very long."

"Nah. He got bound apprentice to Emmanuel last May, and I was already workin there at the shippin company. Emmanuel, he's got this head cooper workin there named Boaz Brooks. Anyway, Boaz has been there decades and he was supposed to train Adam on makin casks and so forth . . ." He took another sip of his drink. "Well, early on they were buttin heads a lot. I was the youngest fella there, so naturally Adam felt comfortable talkin to me. Well . . . that and he's in love with my cousin."

Santiago laughed. "He is in love with your cousin? And this is acceptable to you?"

"What? Adam and my cousin?" Martin wrinkled his brow as though the answer was obvious. "Yeah, it's fine with me. She's a few years older than him. She just turned twenty-one not long before Adam turned eighteen, and she knows how to look out for her best interests. And Adam, he's a good boy—real virtuous and all, not like me."

"I see." Santiago smiled and took a sip of rum from his own flask. "So the two of you have become something like brothers?"

Martin nodded. "Mm-hm. How about either of you? Do you have any brothers or sisters?"

"I'm the youngest of seven children, all boys," Drake replied. "Couldn't wait to get away, so when our father died— and I'm sure he's in Hell right now, miserable drunken lout that he was—I took my share of the inheritance and decided to travel the world. I finally ended up here . . . It took me a while to really settle down, but eventually I fell in love with a local girl and got married, and we just had our first child two years ago—a boy."

"Aw, that's nice," said Martin. "Congratulations. So how about you, Santiago? Any brothers or sisters?"

Santiago shook his head. "No, sadly I was an only child. I would have loved to have grown up with brothers and sisters, though. Most of my friends when I was a young boy had many brothers to play with, and I was very—how you say?—jealous." He took another drink. "But Tomás here, he is like a brother to me."

"That's right," Drake agreed. "In fact, Santiago is the one who first invited me to Havana on the day we met—it was in 1744 in Venice."

Santiago nodded and grinned at the recollection. "Yes, that is right."

"Venice, Italy?" asked Martin.

"That's the only Venice I know anything about," Drake replied.

"What in the world were the two of you doin way over there?"

"We were young men in those days, each of us taking our Grand Tours of Europe. I was coming by way of England, of course, while Santiago here was coming all the way from Havana. There was a very famous composer visiting Venice at the time, and the city was even busier than usual. There was a popular café in the Piazza San Marco, but there weren't many places to sit, so Santiago and I found ourselves seated at the same table—quite uncomfortably, mind you. Anyway, we started to chat a bit, and before long we had passed hours debating international politics, trade, religion, and other such subjects."

"But it was all very civil," Santiago added.

"And you just extended an invitation to him to visit Havana," Martin said to Santiago. "And you took him up on it?" he said to Drake.

"Well, yes. In a roundabout way, of course. A few years passed before I actually made it to Havana."

"I reckon y'all had very different ways of thinkin about things," said Martin. "It's kind of surprising you turned out to be friends."

"That is true," said Santiago. "We had very different views about many things, especially religion, because I am *católico* and Tomás is *protestante*, but the more we conversed, the more we realized that there were other subjects about which we agreed."

"Yes," Drake said, "such as the abuses of power by kings and politicians, regardless of the flag they wave."

Santiago nodded in agreement and handed Drake his flask.

"What is your profession?" Martin asked Drake.

Drake took a drink, then passed the flask back to Santiago and said, "Oh, I do different things. I'm a bit of a jack-of-all-trades, really. I even sailed on *La Dama* once, but I discovered it wasn't something to which I was particularly well suited."

Santiago laughed. "No, it was not."

"What in the world happened?"

"Let's just say I really don't do well at sea. In fact, it's a miracle I made it to Havana in the first place." Drake took another drink. "I can't imagine what I was thinking when I agreed to go with Santiago on one of his expeditions."

"Did you meet my boss, Emmanuel Rogers?" Martin asked Drake.

Drake seemed as though he was thinking, trying to recollect if he had.

Santiago answered for him. "No, he has never met Emmanuel Rogers. Anyway, I have only been to your colony a few times myself, and when Drake joined us on *La Dama*, I do not think we even made it as far as Beaufort."

"Oh, I see," said Martin.

"Probably that's one of the reasons I never have bothered to leave Havana. I'm too sick at sea to make it anywhere anyway, so best I just stay here."

The three of them laughed.

Santiago poked at the fire with a long stick, and there was silence among them for a moment or two. The only thing that could be heard were the waves crashing and the fire crackling.

Martin spoke up and asked Santiago, "So how is it *you* came to know Emmanuel?"

"Emmanuel? I had heard he was looking for someone to supply sugar and Cuban rum, and I was looking for a source for naval stores, and even livestock at one time, so it was beneficial to us both to begin trading with one another."

"Even though it was smugglin?" Martin asked slyly.

Santiago rolled his eyes. "It was business. There are a lot of politics in all of that, and it gives me a headache just to think about it."

Silence again.

"So that's all?" said Martin. He was disappointed. He had hoped there'd be a better story in there somewhere. He took another drink and looked out at the full moon over the ocean, and it appeared to be at its zenith, which meant it was about midnight. He was also starting to feel very relaxed. They still had several hours left before they needed to get into their positions for their plan to foil the bandits, so he thought it would be a good idea to ask Santiago, "You got any pirate blood?"

"What?" Santiago was visibly surprised by the question. "Pirates? No, I do not have any *pirate blood*. At least not that I know anything about, anyway. What a strange question that is to ask!" He took a big swig of rum.

Martin laughed. His speech was becoming more slurred. "Ha-ha. It's not as strange as you might think. A lot of the men back home—especially ones Emmanuel knows—were once involved in piracy one way or another, or they're somehow connected to somebody who was." He threw a piece of wood on the fire, which looked like it was dying down. "My grandfather was a pirate, you know. He sailed with Blackbeard."

"Oh, you are such a liar," Drake countered, chuckling.

"He is joking," said Santiago, laughing. "*El está borracho. The whisky must be turning him into un perico.*" He pinched his fingers up and down to mimic the squawking of a parrot.

"I feel pretty good, but I am not drunk . . . yet . . . and I am not lyin," Martin insisted. "I don't even care if you believe me, though. I know it's the truth."

More silence. All three men looked like they were getting sleepy, but Martin was too anxious to retire for the night. He wanted to keep the conversation going. He asked Santiago another question, even more slurred than the last: "Sooo how does a Cuban captain come to know . . . an English merchant? I mean, I've always wondered how Emmanuel establishes all these contacts of his. He has foreign friends like you all over the place . . ." He started ticking off the fingers on his hand as he said, "I mean France, Hispaniola, St. Maarten, Portugal, Nassau, and so on. In all the time I've known him, he's never traveled anywhere, so I always wonder how he finds you folks."

"Nassau is British," said Drake, laughing. "You really must be drunk."

Martin rolled his eyes at him but turned his attention to Santiago to wait for an answer to his question.

Santiago laughed a bit too, then said, "Ah, well, I know Emmanuel because of my mother."

"Huh? Is your mother English?"

"My mother? Ay, no! She is a proud *española hasta la muerte*—Spanish to the death! But she and my father knew Emmanuel, and when my father died and I decided to visit America, she looked in my father's ledger for the names of his associates and told me I should visit him if I went to North Carolina, that he might have some good contacts for me."

That piqued Martin's curiosity. Now he couldn't help but wonder if Santiago's father might have been one of Emmanuel's friends from his pirating days. He would have to wait before he could probe any further, though. He passed out before he could ask another question.

Chapter Eleven

ADAM FIGURED IT was well after midnight when he started digging again. He had already dealt with two more visits from his captors. He had also kept checking the gaps in the walls so that he could keep an eye on any possible activity happening around the building, but when he was sure that everyone had retired for the night, he wasted no time excavating his way out.

Once he had dug down deep enough and started breaking through to the other side of the wall, he realized that he would have to make his hole extend deeper under the floor mat, or else he wouldn't be able to wiggle his whole body out.

He proceeded to shovel dirt out with his hands, then smooth it out under the mats. On the other side of the wall, he knew he wouldn't be able to smooth the dirt out to hide what he was doing, so the whole time he just prayed he wouldn't get caught.

Finally, he felt like he could get on his belly and start pushing dirt out the other side.

He worked as quickly as he could, until he heard a sound. It was someone stepping on leaves in the distance. Adam debated whether or not he should try to back up into the hut and cover up what he had been doing, or whether he should lie very still and just hope they didn't see him. Circumstances made his decision for him, because as it turned out, he was stuck. He couldn't wiggle forward or backward, so all he could do was hold his breath and pray. *Oh Lord, help me. Help me. Help me. Help me. Help me.*

He heard the stepping on leaves, but it seemed to be getting closer. All of a sudden he made out a scary-looking figure in the shadows, but at least it wasn't human. When the creature was finally illumined as it moved into a beam of moonlight, Adam could make out that it was some gigantic lizard, and he guessed it was one of those animals the Taino Indians called *iwana*. He had heard about them from the men on the *Gypsy* who had visited Cuba before.

Adam had no idea if the thing would come over to where he was, if it would bite, or if it was poisonous, but for the moment at least his fear of the giant lizard paled in comparison to his fear of getting caught by Hector or one of his fellow kidnappers.

He kept digging, digging, digging and pushing out dirt and digging, until finally he was able to wiggle his way completely out of the hole.

Just then he heard the voices of two men talking from the other side of the building that he thought was the common room. *Oh, no . . . I thought everybody was asleep.*

Adam couldn't worry about that right now, though. He

had to make a run for it, or he'd lose his chance. He hesitated only long enough to listen for the sound of the ocean and get his bearings straight. He took off running quietly for the loud, crashing waves. Just as he entered back into the forest that surrounded the compound, he heard voices yelling from around the hut where he had escaped. *They must realize I'm gone.* He kept running but soon heard a multitude of men shouting, calling out what sounded like instructions to one another.

"Thank you, God!" Adam exclaimed out loud as the beach came into view.

Adam picked up his speed. He knew if he could make it there, he would stand a better chance of having a clean escape.

Suddenly, he heard footsteps running a good distance behind him and the thunderous crack of a pistol firing. That meant they saw him and were after him. He better forget about running to the beach now. Being out in the open would mean he'd be caught for sure. He veered back into the forest and prayed the darkness and foliage would give him enough cover to find a place to hide.

Chapter Twelve

THE TORREON DE la Chorrera—named for the river on which a torreon, or tower, had been originally constructed more than a century earlier—was located on a tiny peninsula that jutted out into the mouth of the Chorrera river.

After the men who were camping out in the tower had slept a few hours, they were all awakened by Drake, who was eager to get everyone into their positions. He had been involved in operations like this in the past and knew it was best to start earlier than seemed necessary and be prepared rather than start just in time and miss something important.

"Get up, you lot! The sun will be up in a little more than an hour, so we must start movin to our positions."

In spite of only having had a little bit of sleep, Charlie, Santiago, and the others didn't waste time getting up and gathering the supplies they needed to put their plan into action. Martin was moving a little slower, but he was still feeling groggy from all that whisky he drank.

Not all of the men would need to leave the tower right away, but they would all need to be ready to keep an eye out for the signal.

Drake had devised a scheme whereby Martin, Charlie, and Santiago would be posted in hidden locations at equidistant positions around a shrine of the Virgin Mary about a hundred yards from the tower. (That was the place indicated on the ransom letter as the delivery point.) They wanted to be sure that no matter which direction the man, or men, came from to pick up the ransom, they would be able to see where he, or they, went so that they could stay on his trail. They figured out a way to do this by sending back reflected light signals for the others to follow using pocket mirrors or whatever shiny metals they were able to use.

There would be sixteen possible signals to indicate the direction as specifically as possible, ranging from one flash to sixteen flashes and working their way around a sixteen-point compass rose, starting with the northern position. So one flash meant north, two meant north-northeast, three meant northeast, four meant east northeast, and so on. As soon as the ransom was collected by the "money man," whoever was nearest the direction in which he began to travel would flash a signal with the direction—first to the tower, where Drake would be waiting—then flash to the men posted at the other two locations, since they likely would not have seen where the money man went.

The first person who flashed the signal—the one closest to the money man—would quietly begin to follow him on foot for as far as he was able, and then the others would trickle in behind him on horseback, or by boat if necessary, continually signaling behind them to any other men following to ensure that they were able to move quietly and in a staggered fashion.

Just a few minutes before the break of day, the servant from the Velasquez family estate came to deliver the ransom money. He looked all around with great curiosity to see if he could see anyone coming, then placed the sack of coins behind the statue of the Virgin Mary, inside the shrine. As he walked away, he looked back to see if anyone was coming to collect it, just as he had been told to do, and then he got back into the boat in which he had come and sailed back towards the town.

Once he had sailed almost completely out of sight, two men appeared and approached the shrine, presumably to collect the money. They had come from the south-southwest, along the eastern bank of the Chorrera River. That meant Martin was closest to their position, since he was waiting near a small fishing boat in the Chorrera that was hidden in a little grotto of tropical foliage to the northwest of the shrine.

As soon as he saw the money men leaving with the ransom, he sent a signal of ten flashes, meaning south-southwest, to Drake in the tower. Drake quickly signaled back with two long flashes, indicating that he had received the message. Drake then conveyed the signal to the other men waiting nearby. So far things were going exactly according to plan.

Martin rowed his boat down the river a bit so that he could continue observing the money men. After a short time they got into their own little boat and crossed the river to the west side, then got out and started down a path along the riverbank before crossing into the woods.

Realizing Martin was the one in the best position to follow the men, Santiago had followed his movements at a safe distance along the eastern edge of the river on horseback, until he, too, saw the men enter the forest. He quickly rode back to the shrine, where he was met by Drake and Charlie and the others, and he explained to them what he had seen.

It frustrated everyone to know the men hadn't just ventured southward or eastward. That meant that now some of them would either have to ride south along the river's edge until they came to a shallow crossing, or they would have to swim their horses across the wide stretch of the river nearby. Both were bad options, since the longer it took them to cross, the farther ahead Martin would be, making it difficult for them to follow.

Jones, Canady, and Willis volunteered to stay by the fort, while Drake, Santiago, and Charlie decided to ride south until they could find a stretch of river that seemed shallow enough that the horses wouldn't have to swim across. Their main concern would be keeping their pistols and powder dry in the crossing.

Within a few minutes they all made it across the river without incident and were soon approaching the place where Santiago had seen the money men enter the woods, followed by Martin. Unfortunately, though, their targets had all already progressed so far along the forest path that they were no longer visible. Santiago and company could only hope that traveling on horseback would quickly get them caught up. Still, they needed to move as quietly as possible so that the money men would not hear them when they did catch up.

Soon they could see ahead that the path ended at a road that either led eastward back to the city or westward, presumably towards their destination. Santiago rode forward slowly and looked both ways but saw no evidence of Martin or the money men. Assuming they had probably traveled west, he continued looking in that direction when he thought he saw a flash far ahead in the trees. He rode that way for a short distance and motioned for the others to follow him. After that he saw the flash again. Judging from the distance, he guessed that Martin was about a mile ahead.

The three of them quickly rode in that direction, with Santiago keeping a lookout for more signals, but there were none. Unfortunately, the vegetation along the road was getting thicker, so Santiago guessed that Martin was unable to catch enough sunlight on his mirror anymore to create the signal flashes. They would have to hope he had left some clues behind to mark his trail.

There was nothing along the road near where Santiago thought he had seen the flash.

"Stupid Martin!" he exclaimed. "He left nothing here for us to follow."

Drake circled around in front of Santiago, then said, "Not so fast, amigo. This is where you think you saw him, on the right side of the road?"

Santiago nodded.

Drake dismounted his horse and started closely examining the area. He looked at the ground, the branches, the vines, and leaves, everything. "They went this way."

"*¿Como sabes?*" asked Santiago.

"How do I know?" Drake laughed. "Must you even ask?"

He stroked his young stallion's mane and then grabbed the saddle horn and pulled himself back up and started riding, then motioned for the others to follow him.

As they rode into the forest, Drake pointed out things he had noticed. "The ground here looks trod upon. The branches have been pushed back. And up ahead"—he pointed farther into the woods—"I think I see something on that shrub."

Sure enough, when they reached what looked like a

shrub, they realized that it was actually a tightly clumped cluster of vines. Tied to one of the serpentine stems was a small strip of fabric that Martin must've cut off his clothing with his knife.

"This is all very strange," said Santiago. "We are in the middle of nowhere. Why would these men be trying so hard to hide their trail? Who would even see it? We are far from the main road."

At that point the trail became more apparent. It was the same hidden forest path that Hector and Carlos had taken Adam on, but Martin was making no effort to cover over his steps and was bending back branches as he was able to in hopes of marking the trail for his friends. He would have broken branches but it would have made too much noise.

Unfortunately, however, Martin did break a branch, but it was underfoot and was definitely not done intentionally.

The cracking sound echoed through the forest. Suddenly, voices could be faintly detected in the distance. They were so far away it sounded like mumbling. Martin realized they must've heard the noise from the branch, and he was torn as to whether he should still try to pursue them alone, or whether he'd be better off waiting for the others to catch up on horseback. His decision was made for him when Santiago, Drake, and Charlie suddenly came tearing through the forest, Santiago stopping just long enough to pull him up onto his horse with him, and they took off in the direction of the voices. Soon the money men were visible ahead of them. They took off running, calling out continually in Spanish.

Before long they could see the grass-thatched roofs of the fortress huts emerging from the tops of the trees and wondered how many men they would have to fight to rescue Adam. As soon as they came upon the compound, they were surprised to see the place looked like it was nearly abandoned. The money men must've gotten there and warned whoever their boss was, causing them to disappear back into the forest.

AFTER QUICKLY EXPLORING THE compound, Martin, Santiago, Drake, and Charlie were satisfied that the place had indeed been abandoned—at least temporarily.

As soon as they saw the building that looked like some kind of cell, they unbolted the door and went inside, hoping to find Adam, but he was not there. There was only a frail-looking man chained to the wall.

"What do you mean he is not here?" Santiago demanded of him in Spanish as Drake worked on picking the lock that held the man chained to the wall.

The prisoner explained what had happened the night before. Drake translated the conversation for Martin and Charlie. He told them that Adam was able to dig himself out and run away, but then he heard men running after him and guns firing, and he did not know whether Adam made it out of the forest alive.

"Damnit all!" Martin exclaimed. "That sounds just like Adam Fletcher. Impatient and always takin matters into his own hands. And he always ends up gettin himself into trouble! Damn!" He stomped the ground and turned away in frustration.

"But he survives," said Charlie. "He seems to be able to take care of himself alright."

Santiago asked the prisoner a question, and he responded, waving his hand in a northerly direction.

"What'd he say?" Martin asked.

"He says they went north, towards the beach," answered Drake.

"The beach?" said Charlie, perplexed. "We're near the beach?"

Santiago and the prisoner exchanged a few more words, then Santiago said, "Yes. He says he has not been to it from here—of course, he has been imprisoned—but he says you can hear it if you listen carefully, especially at night when everything is quiet. It sounds like it is a little bit in that direction." He waved his hand northward.

Drake rolled his eyes. "Those stealthy devils! They've had us on a wild-goose chase!"

He continued to work on picking the lock.

Santiago took a deep breath in frustration, then exhaled sharply. "I believe you are right, my friend." He thought for a moment, then said, "Martin, you come with me, and we will search for him near the beach. Drake, will you be able to get this man freed?"

"I should have this lock sorted out any second now," Drake answered. "I'll catch up to you in a minute."

Santiago, Martin, and Charlie ran through the camp and north towards where the man said the beach was. As they got closer, they could hear the waves.

Santiago pointed out boot marks in the ground, which they all followed until the path became too leafy. Soon they came to the beach, but there was no evidence of which way Adam could have gone. Naturally, they assumed he would have gone east.

Martin said, "If they were firin their pistols at him, I doubt he would have stayed out here in the open. He prob'ly turned back to take cover in the woods."

"And that means he could be anywhere," said Charlie.

"How many miles do you reckon we are from that river?" Martin asked Santiago.

"I do not know. We went so far in those woods, we could be a very short distance from that river or a very long distance."

"So what do we do now?" asked Charlie.

"Let me think for a moment."

Santiago walked onto the beach and looked out on the sea. The shore was rocky, and there was forest as far as he could see in either direction. Because the beach curved outwards, he could not determine how far they were from where they had been, but he guessed it couldn't be too far.

"Santiago! Get over here and see this," Martin called out.

He walked back over to where Martin and Charlie were standing. "What is it?"

"Look," said Charlie. He pointed to a tree with what appeared to be blood that had been smeared on it and then dried.

Santiago looked at the mark, then looked around and noticed a few other trees appeared to have blood on them. But then the trail disappeared. There were no more blood-marked trees that he or the others could find.

"What does this even mean?" said Charlie.

Just then Drake ran over to join them. "What does what mean?" he said, out of breath.

"Look," said Martin, pointing to the trees with the blood. "Somebody was bleedin here, and my guess is it was Adam."

"Oh Lord, you're right!" Charlie grimaced. "The guys who were after him had guns and who knows what all else. He had nothing except maybe that pitiful little pocketknife that he carries with him everywhere."

"We better find him! He could be gravely injured," Santiago exclaimed.

He started walking fast and hard back towards the camp.

Martin and Charlie exchanged worried glances and quickly followed after him.

Santiago stopped in his tracks. "Wait, what's that? Do you hear? Over by the camp?"

The other three men stopped moving and held still and silent.

Santiago said, "They are shouting commands—like an army or militia." He hushed everybody by holding up his hand. After a moment he said, "I think I understand what this is, and if I am right, this is much worse than I thought."

Now they were all suddenly wishing they hadn't left the other three men from the *Gypsy* back at the tower.

"What is it?" asked Drake.

"It is a trap, but I don't have time to explain. Wait here."

Just then Santiago ran ahead into the fortress with his hands up, shouting out in Spanish, "*¿Donde está el comandante? ¡Soy su sobrino!*"

Drake translated to Martin and Charlie. "He just asked for the commander of this place."

"Who is the commander?" asked Charlie.

Drake raised his eyebrows and said, "Apparently, he's Santiago's uncle."

"What!" Martin exclaimed. "What kind of people are these?!"

"Apparently, they're crazy, violent ones," answered Charlie.

Chapter Thirteen

*H*OW MANY TIMES *does a man have to spend the night hiding out in forests to avoid crazed killers?* Adam wondered what the chances were that he was now finding himself in similar circumstances to the ones he had experienced last year when he had to hide out from those men on the island where he had been marooned.

It really didn't matter. The fact was he was going to do what he needed to do to make it through the night and get back to the port in Havana. He had serious misgivings about Hector and company even having the wherewithal to find the right ship and crew so they could demand their ransom. Even if they had gotten their message through, he wasn't confident that Captain Phillips and company would be able to get whatever money was being demanded by his captors in the specified time. And finally, at this point he really just wanted to get out of this tropical hell and make it back home.

Furthermore, it did not escape him that yet again, because of his impatience he had gotten himself into trouble. If he had only waited for Martin or insisted someone else go with him, this whole thing probably would have never happened.

Nevertheless, although he had gotten far enough ahead of the gunmen that he no longer heard them running after him, he still had no idea how far he was from the Havana port. He only knew that he was heading east because he had seen the sunrise not too much earlier.

When he finally came to a bay that appeared to be the mouth of a large river emptying into the sea, he wondered if it was the same one he had crossed the day before with Hector and Carlos in the horse cart. It was hard to be sure, since the waterway from the day before was so narrow—almost like a little stream—and shallow enough for the cart to go right across in one section. If it was the same river, then he guessed that he couldn't be more than four or five miles from the quay where the *Gypsy* was moored.

It looked like the area across the bay used to be some sort of military fortification. There were stonework walls all around and in the distance what looked like a hewn-stone tower that had apparently been bombarded with cannon fire. Upon further observation he noticed the waterway quickly narrowed just a little to the south, so he ran along the water's edge until he knew he could swim across quickly and easily.

Once he was on the other side, he headed north again for the shoreline. He knew if he just kept following it, he would end up back at the port in about an hour and a half.

As he neared the tower he had seen, he found it curious

that there seemed to be a few men sitting there around a fire cooking something. He had traveled quite a distance without seeing another living soul, and now all of a sudden here were men cooking actual food. When he realized that he recognized them, he wondered if the whole thing might just be a mirage. *This can't be real*, he thought. *This is too good to be true.*

"Hey! Willis! Canady! Jones! Is that really you?" he called out as he got close to the men.

The three of them looked at each other, then quickly looked to see who was calling them. As he got closer, Adam was sure they were his shipmates. The tallest one, sandy-haired Ed Willis, stood up and approached Adam. The rough-looking redhead, Fred Canady, and the raven-haired Englishman, Ricky Jones, followed close behind him.

"Good Lord, man!" Willis exclaimed. "The whole wide world is out lookin for you right now."

"What?" said Adam. "Who is?"

"You look like hell," Canady remarked.

Adam rolled his eyes. "I feel like hell. Long story. Who's out looking for me? And what are you boys doing here?"

"Some chap showed up on the *Gypsy* yesterday, bringin a note demandin ransom. Said if we didn't pay up, they'd kill you," said Jones. "Cap'n Phillips had Martin and Charlie go get this Spanish fellow he knows to help out. Name's Velasquez. Anyhow, he and this other man—English chap named Drake, I think— and Martin and Charlie, they all went chasin down the men who picked up the ransom this morning."

"Yep. They wanted to follow 'em back to their hideout to rescue you," said Canady.

"Y'all paid the ransom?" asked Adam.

"Of course! Well, somebody did. I think it was actually that Spanish captain," said Willis.

"Captain Velasquez . . ." Adam thought hard. "Wasn't he that Spanish captain from—what was it called? . . . Oh, I can't remember the name of the ship. Anyway, I think he was in Beaufort last year, at Laney's estate."

"I think they were sayin that's him, yeah," said Willis. "I hadn't met him before, though."

Adam must have looked like he was about to collapse, because his three shipmates insisted he sit down and eat some of what they had been cooking. But he didn't want to sit. He wanted to find his friends Martin and Charlie and those other two men. Still, he realized he hadn't eaten anything since the meal he had at the outdoor café the day before. He'd given his piece of bread to the chained prisoner back at the compound.

He decided to accept his friends' invitation to eat so he could fortify himself. Then he'd lead the others to the camp where he had been held. He hated thinking his friends were putting themselves in harm's way when he had already escaped. And as much as he still wanted answers, at this point he wished he had just listened to his mother and not bothered trying to find out anything about his father. It had brought him nothing but misfortune from the start. Maybe it just was not meant to be.

AFTER SCARFING DOWN A quick meal, Adam stood from the broken piece of stone wall upon which he was sitting and said to his friends, "Alright, I'm done. Let's go."

"Ya sure about that, mate?" asked Jones. "You ain't slept all night. This is the first meal you've eaten since yesterday morning.

Maybe you should rest here. Sketch us out a map and show us where to go."

"Yeah," Willis agreed. "Why don't you do that? You don't seem like you're in any condition to be going anywhere."

Adam didn't bother answering either of them. He went over to the bags of gear that he'd learned were inside the tower and grabbed a .50 flintlock pistol and a leather satchel of gear. He also grabbed a machete and a holster for his belt.

"What the devil are you doin, mate?" asked Jones.

"What does it look like I'm doing?" Adam yelled in response as he purposefully strode back to the point in the river where he had crossed earlier. "Come with me or stay here, but I'm going back to that compound."

"What about the horses?" asked Willis.

Adam stopped for a minute and turned back, realizing his shipmates planned to come along. "Forget about 'em. That place ain't too far. We can get there easier on foot. Now hurry up if you're comin!"

Jones and Willis grabbed pistols and gear, and Canady agreed to go back to the *Gypsy* to let the captain know what was happening. In no time Adam, Jones, and Willis were fording the river and heading back towards the beach.

Chapter Fourteen

UPON ARRIVING AT the grove of Kapok trees where he had come out of the woods hours earlier, Adam remembered the sounds of the men chasing after him, deafening gunshots cracking the silence. He thought about his friends and the danger they could be in, and he was struck with a surge of adrenaline.

"Follow me, but keep quiet," he told Willis and Jones. "We're less than a mile away now, but they could still have men on the lookout."

The three of them moved quietly through the woods. When Adam heard voices in the distance, he held up his hand, motioning for the other two to stop.

"Just listen," he said to them.

The three were silent for a moment. Adam looked at

Willis and Jones, who both shrugged, unable to make out much of what or who they were hearing.

"How are we gonna do this?" Jones asked in a nervous whisper.

"Very quietly," said Adam. "We don't even know if our men are in there. We need to scout the place out first."

"Go ahead, then," whispered Willis. "We'll follow behind you."

Adam nodded.

They crept through the forest with stealth and speed. Soon the fortress was visible. Adam motioned for Willis and Jones to come near.

"There it is, boys," he said.

"So what's the plan, mate?" asked Jones.

"Let me think for a minute," said Adam. He looked back over towards the fortress, studying it carefully as best he could from a distance. It looked like there were armed men outside the hut that he was told belonged to the leader of the operation.

He turned his attention back to his friends. "Our men could be here, but even if they're not, the leader of this outfit must be, because there are guards posted outside his hut."

"Do you have a strategy in mind?" asked Willis.

Adam sighed in exhaustion. He was tired, but he didn't have time to think about that right now. "Yeah. I'm going to get closer to those buildings to see if I can figure out if Martin and the others are in there."

"And you think you can evade those armed guards?" Jones asked.

"Lord willing," said Adam. "If you can, just keep an eye out and signal to me if it looks like anyone is heading in my direction."

"You're crazy," Willis whispered sharply. "You're goin to walk right into this armed compound? And then what? What if our fellas are in there? What kind of damage are just the three of us gonna be able to do?"

"Well, we'll just have to cross that bridge if and when we get to it."

"Listen, Fletcher, at least Jones and I have been in the militia," said Willis. He motioned to the pistol Adam was carrying. "Have you ever even fired one of those?"

"Of course I have," insisted Adam. "But I expect I'll do a lot better with this." He clutched the hilt of the machete he had at his side.

"You damn sure better hope so, mate," said Jones. "Remind me again why we don't just go to the Cuban authorities about this."

Adam narrowed his eyes in disbelief at Jones's question. "The Cuban authorities? First of all, we just smuggled in hundreds of pounds' worth of merchandise the day before yesterday. To make matters worse, you went and asked the high sheriff of this place for his recommendation on a place to drink—and he turned up there and ate with us!"

Adam stepped back, exasperated, and ran his fingers through his hair while exhaling sharply. Jones stood there looking at him, waiting to see if he'd say any more.

Adam continued: "Anyway, he already seemed suspicious, like he had his eye on us—and I reckon it's probably because of whatever trouble y'all got into last time you were here!" He poked Jones in the chest. "The last thing we need to do now is run to him and tell him we've gotten into a mess like this. There's no telling what might come out of that, and we sure don't want him poking around in our shipping manifests and cockets."

"Say no more." Jones threw his hands up in surrender to Adam's argument. "I understand." He looked at Willis and commented, "He sure does have a quick temper, this kid, eh?"

Willis just raised his eyebrow and chuckled.

"We're going to have to work this out for ourselves, boys," said Adam. "And if we don't do it right, we're going to really make a mess of things."

Adam led Willis and Jones around the fortress to the other side so that he could approach from behind the leader's hut. As far as he knew, there was only one door to the place, and the armed guards were standing in front of it.

He figured there was no need to bother with going too near the common room. If Martin and the others had been there and not made it out again, chances were they were locked up in the prison hut. That would be the first place he would check.

WILLIS AND JONES HID in the dense vegetation on the eastern edge of the fortress, but with a clear view to watch Adam as he crept into the compound.

As he neared the prison hut, he hid behind a stone well that was just outside, and he listened. There were voices coming from inside. *That has to be Martin and Charlie*, Adam thought. He crept closer and looked through the logs that formed one of the walls. He was able to see inside. It *was* Martin and Charlie, but there was another man in there, too. From what he could tell, his accent was English, so he assumed it was the man they called Drake.

Adam quickly considered whether he should get Willis and Jones to come over and help. He didn't want to risk running out in the open again, so he opted to just motion to them and point to the building, hoping they could figure out that he was trying to tell them the others were inside.

"Psst!" he whispered loudly through the crack in the wall. No one seemed to notice or hear him, so he picked up a pebble from the ground and flicked it through the crack as best he could. It hit Charlie on the cheek.

"What in the world?" Charlie said, then looked up to see if whatever had just hit him could have come from the ceiling.

Adam flicked another pebble, but this time Charlie looked in his direction, since he could apparently tell it had come from one of the cracks in the wall. Charlie, Martin, and Drake all scurried across the floor of the hut and peered between the logs.

"Adam!" Martin exclaimed. "How'd you get here?"

"Does it matter? Listen, Willis and Jones are here with me. Canady has gone back to the *Gypsy* to let the captain know where we are. We're going to get y'all out."

"We'll be fine, but you need to get out of here!" said Drake. "I'm Thomas Drake, by the way. Nice to meet you."

"Likewise," said Adam. "What do you mean you'll be fine? You're locked in a prisoner's hut in Middle-of-Nowhere, Cuba!"

Martin answered before anyone else had a chance to say anything. "Because Captain Velasquez is here, and he's in with the leader right now negotiatin for our release." He shot a stern look at Charlie and Drake.

Adam wrinkled his brow. "I saw that! You're up to something. What is it?"

"You might as well tell him," said Drake. "He should know."

"Now's not the time," insisted Martin.

"Now's not the time for what?" said a frustrated Adam.

"He's rash and impatient and tends to go off half-cocked,

so I'm tellin you: do not tell him!" Martin made a stern, insistent face.

Drake rolled his eyes at Martin, then looked at Adam and said, "Fine, I'll tell you."

Martin and Charlie both looked at Drake like they could kill him.

"The thing is," said Drake, "turns out that Santiago—I mean Captain Velasquez—knows the leader of this whole outfit. They've had a run-in before."

Martin and Charlie both let out a deep breath. Adam could tell that Drake had apparently only given him half of the story, but it did seem to change the dynamics of the situation a bit. Only he didn't know how. Would it make things better or worse that Captain Velasquez knew the man in charge? Was Captain Velasquez even someone who could be trusted?"

Suddenly, they could all hear someone call something out in Spanish from not far away.

"They know you're back," said Drake. "You better run!"

Adam looked towards the north end of the hut, and a man was running straight at him. He ran to the southern end in an effort to get away. He had barely turned the corner when another man came around it at the same time and caught him, grabbing him firmly by his shoulders.

"¡Ya lo tengo!" the man cried out.

Adam reached for his machete, but the other man—who clearly had much more experience with the blades—fearlessly snatched it away from him by grabbing the dull edge, then tossed it out of reach. Still, Adam was able to pull himself from the man's grip and started to run again, but he didn't make it far before he was tackled by two other men.

Within moments they had taken his pistol and tossed him into the prison hut, along with the others.

"WHERE'S THE FELLOW WHO was chained up?" asked Adam.

"He's gone," said Drake.

Adam's eyes grew enormous. "What happened to him?"

"We let him go when we got here this mornin," said Martin.

"And then we got caught," said Charlie.

"I can see that." Adam rolled his eyes and quickly crossed the room and peeled back the floor mats to look for where he had dug the hole in the floor the night before.

"What in the world are you doin, boy?" asked Martin.

"Oh, that's just great!" Adam threw the mat back down onto the floor. "They filled up the hole."

"You said Willis and Jones are with you. Where are they?" asked Charlie.

"In those woods over there," said Adam, motioning to the forest across the field from the western side of the hut. "That is, unless they saw what happened and took off."

"Ah, I very much doubt they'd do that," said Drake. "I believe those boys both said last night they were trained in the militia. I don't believe either of them is the type who'd cut and run."

"Well, what can a militia of two do?" asked Adam.

"If they're clever, you'd be surprised," Drake answered.

The four of them stood in silence for a moment, contemplating the situation. Finally, Martin asked Adam, "You got that knife of yours with you?"

He thought for a second, then squatted down, but just

before he was about to reach into his boot to pull it out, the door to the prison hut was flung open, and two guards came inside, along with Hector, the man who had originally kidnapped Adam the day before.

"You," he said, pointing at Adam, "and you"—he pointed at Drake. "The *comandante* is wanting to seeing you in his *salón*."

"Why does he want to see you?" Martin asked Drake.

Drake shrugged. "I've no idea. Just be glad he does."

ADAM'S AND DRAKE'S HANDS were bound in front of them, and they were marched into the leader's hut.

Upon seeing them enter the room, Santiago exclaimed, "*¡Gracias a Dios!*"

Adam gave a quizzical look at Drake. He had no idea what the Spanish captain was saying, other than that he was saying thank you about something. Then he realized the mustachioed man sitting at the desk in the hut, the *comandante*, was the same man he had met at the Taberna El Trobador, the high sheriff.

"What is this? Are we under arrest or something?" he asked, too stunned to say anything else.

Drake looked around the room and appeared to be taking stock of the situation. He looked at Santiago, who told him something in Spanish, which caused Drake to roll his eyes and exhale sharply in exasperation.

"*Que bueno.* Finally, we are all here together." The sheriff sat back in his chair with a smug look on his face and not one ounce of sincerity.

Santiago said something to the man that Adam could not understand, but he appeared to be very emotional.

"Don't beg the rotten bastard," said Drake. "The others will be here soon, and he'll be the one begging us for mercy."

"You are Adam?" Santiago said, looking right at him.

"Yeah," he nodded. "That's me."

Santiago's expression demonstrated both his relief and his fear. "Thank God you are fine," he said, then turned his attention back to the mustachioed man. "Let him go. This has nothing to do with him."

"What do you mean, this has nothing to do with me? Why would any of this have anything to do with me?" asked Adam.

The sheriff reached into a box on his desk and took out a cigar. He ran it under his nose to inhale the fragrance, then grabbed a little blade from under a stack of papers on his desk and cut the end. After using his thumb to dust away any loose tobacco from the cut end, he moistened it in his mouth. Next he grabbed a thin piece of wood from his desk and lit it using the flame from a little lamp that was there. He brought the lit piece of wood up to the tip of the cigar and twisted it in his mouth as he puffed to get it going.

"I have wondered if this day would come for more than eighteen years." He took a draw from his cigar and held it in his mouth for a couple of seconds before he exhaled. Then he lowered the cigar and said, "I had hoped circumstances would never come to this, but here we are."

Now Adam was really confused. He looked at Drake for some explanation.

Drake looked at Santiago with a worried look in his eyes. "Santiago . . . You should—"

"I reckon this means you're not really the *high sheriff* like you said you were, huh?" Adam asked.

"Yes, he is," said Santiago.

The mustachioed man puffed on his cigar. He appeared to be relishing the confusion.

"What's going on here?" said Adam. "What kind of sheriff kidnaps somebody for ransom?"

The sheriff laughed. "Do you think that is really what this is about?"

Adam stood there expressionless and said nothing.

"This is not about ransom," said the man. "This was only . . . a distraction, you could say. If my stupid nephew here had not involved himself, and if you had only stayed in the cell until the ransom was collected and we delivered you back to your vessel, you would already be on your way back to your young lady in North Carolina."

"So what'd you kidnap me for, then?" Adam demanded.

"Do you know who that man is sitting there in that chair?" asked the sheriff, motioning with the hand that was not holding the cigar.

Adam turned his head towards Santiago, and then he looked back at the sheriff and said, "He's a captain and your nephew, and apparently he helped my friends try to find me. That's all I know about him."

"His name is Santiago Velasquez," said the sheriff. "My name is Eduardo Velasquez."

"So? You're related. I don't care what your name is," said Adam. "You are nothing to me."

Eduardo laughed. "You are right, *chico*, but you do not even know why that is true." He placed the cigar into an ashtray on his desk and slightly leaned forward on his elbows. "Tell me something: Who were you looking for when you came to Havana?"

Adam wrinkled his brow. "Why?"

"*You* do not ask me questions now. *I* am asking the questions."

"What if I don't answer your questions? Because frankly I don't think it's any of your business what I was doing or who I was looking for when I came here."

Just then Eduardo nodded his head at one of the men guarding Drake, and he came down hard on the side of Drake's knee with the butt of his rifle. Drake collapsed in pain as his leg went out from under him.

Adam watched what happened in horror and tried to lunge forward to help Drake, but Hector grabbed him and yanked him backwards.

"Now you will answer me," said Eduardo.

Adam clearly resented having to answer, but he did. "I was looking for a man called Alonso Cordova."

"And why were you looking for this man?"

"My grandfather knows him."

"Your *grandfather?*" Eduardo leaned back in his chair and puffed on his cigar again. "How does your *grandfather* know him?"

Adam shrugged. "He just told me I should look for him while I am here."

Eduardo slammed his palm on his desk and yelled, "You are lying!"

"I am not lying!" said Adam. "How would you know what my grandfather told me?"

"What is the name of your grandfather?"

Adam would not answer. He didn't want to lie, and he knew he wasn't very good at it anyway. Valentine wasn't really his grandfather, but he was the closest thing to a grandfather that he ever had.

Eduardo said, "His name is Valentine Hodges, is it not? And he is the proprietor of the Topsail Tavern in Port Beaufort, correct?"

The color left Adam's face. He had no idea how or why this Cuban sheriff would know so much about him.

Santiago interjected something in Spanish.

Eduardo raised his hand to silence him, then said to Adam, "You know, you should not even be alive. Your mother was supposed to die in the fire at that tavern before you were even born. The truth is I did not know she was with child, but since she was carrying you in her belly at the time, you would have died with her. That would have been so much easier"—he waved his hands around in the air—"than all of *this*."

"You are an evil man!" Santiago tried to bolt out of his chair to fly at his uncle, but the man behind him shoved him back down. In response Hector reached from behind Adam and put his arm around his neck. Then he held a knife to the boy's throat in an apparent effort to prevent Santiago from having another similar outburst.

Santiago quickly stopped trying to bust free, then turned and said to Hector, "You always were a traitor. Does it make you proud?"

Hector lowered the knife, then looked at him and shrugged. "Proud? I not feeling proud, but it is paying very well."

Adam narrowed his eyes at Eduardo. "I heard about a fire at the tavern the summer the Spaniards from Florida attacked our port—the year before I was born. You started that fire?"

"Stupid boy," said Eduardo. "I have never set foot in your

tiny village, but you might be surprised what other men will do for thirty pieces of silver . . . or even less."

Santiago spoke up. "My Tio Eduardo helped to finance the final attack on your town that summer, Adam. And it was because that man—the one standing right there behind you—abandoned my ship and came back to Cuba so that he could betray me."

Adam was visibly puzzled. "I don't understand what any of you people are talking about. Would you please just tell me what is going on?"

"Hector was a member of my crew," said Santiago, "as was Alonso Cordova." He took a deep breath and looked at Adam as though he were waiting for some response.

Adam wrinkled his brow, not sure he heard what he thought he heard.

"Adam, *soy tu papá.*"

The room fell silent. No one even moved a muscle.

Santiago said it again, his voice cracking, but in English. "I am your father, Adam."

Adam suddenly felt very hot, like he was going to be sick. His heart was pounding, and his head felt light. *He didn't just say what I think he just said?* He looked over at Drake, who was now crumpled in a chair, for some reaction. Drake gave him a slight smile and a nod. Adam looked back at Santiago, unsure of whether this was all some sort of elaborate scheme.

Santiago's hands weren't bound like Adam's. He was about to stand so he could rush over and embrace the boy, but as soon as he started to rise from his chair, the man standing behind him pushed him forcefully back down into his seat again.

"Wait a minute," said Adam, utterly dumbfounded. "Is this true?" He looked at Eduardo, then back at Santiago.

Santiago said, "Yes, I swear it to you that it is the truth. It was days after I married your mother on *La Dama* that Hector disappeared. Apparently, my uncle told him before he joined my crew to keep an eye on me and to let him know if I ever became very serious with any woman outside of Cuba."

"You married my mother?" Adam asked. "She really was married to you?"

Santiago nodded. "Of course. How else do you think we made you?"

Adam could hear his heart beating in his ears. He was so angry he didn't know what to say. Finally, it occurred to him to ask a question.

"Then where in the hell have you been the last eighteen years?"

Santiago lowered his head. "It is a long story and—"

"It is not such a long story," countered Eduardo, who then looked at Adam. "You only need to know that if he had made it apparent that you existed, that he had a son, he feared I would have killed you long ago." He made that declaration with such calm that it sent a chill down Adam's spine. Eduardo continued: "He was trying to hide you from me."

Adam ignored him. He turned his attention to Santiago. "But we met just last year. Don't you remember?"

"Yes, of course I remember!" Santiago exclaimed, smiling. "You had no money, and I gave you a bag of little *regalitos* from my ship."

"Why didn't you say anything then?"

Santiago shook his head in bewilderment. "I did not say anything then because I did not know it myself. I only realized you were my son when your friends came to ask for my help finding you. They said your mother's name, and that you had come here trying to find Alonso, so I knew it had to be you. I never—"

"¡*Basta*! ¡*Ya*!" interrupted Eduardo.

He then spat out something in Spanish to Santiago that Adam was not able to understand. He could see that Santiago was outraged by whatever had been said, though, because his face turned red, and his eyes were fixed on the man with fury. Soon, Santiago and Eduardo were engaged in a heated argument that involved a lot of yelling, hand waving, and finger pointing.

"You are both blind, obviously," said Eduardo. "Look at you both!" He motioned at Santiago and Adam. "He looks just like you!"

Adam looked at Santiago, but then said, "I look like my mother."

"You do look like me," said Santiago. "Just like me when I was young like you."

"But he looks nothing like my brother," said Eduardo, motioning to Santiago. "And that is because he is *not* my brother's son."

"¡*Bastardo*!" Santiago roared, then rattled off something in Spanish. He turned to Adam and said, "He is consumed with greed because I am in line to receive my father's estate—the Velasquez family estate."

"What does that have to do with me?" Adam shot back.

"Stupid boy!" said Eduardo. "If he is your father and he is to inherit what does not rightfully belong to him, then you would be next in line—and I will not have it!"

"Why do you say it doesn't rightfully belong to him?" Adam asked.

"Because he is Isabel's bastard son. He is *not* my brother's son."

"You say this all the time." Santiago grabbed the hair on both sides of his head in frustration. "Why do you always say this?"

"*¡Deberías haber preguntado a tu madre!*" Eduardo insisted. "You should have asked your mother!"

Finally, Adam spoke up. "If you're worried about me wanting a piece of this godforsaken island, there's no need. Trust me. There's nothing here that I want."

Eduardo responded in Spanish, and Santiago promptly translated. "He says that's only because you do not know all that you would come to possess through our family's great fortune."

"Is that so?" said Adam. "You know nothing! The Velasquez family could own this whole damned island and all of the Spanish West Indies, and I still wouldn't care. If being part of the Velasquez family means I'd have you for an uncle—a man willing to kidnap or even kill his own nephew because of his greed, his love of money—I'd want no part in any of it." He paused for a second, then added, "I'd be ashamed to claim you. You're an embarrassment."

Eduardo got up from his chair and walked around his desk to Adam and stood right in front of him, studying him for a moment. Finally, without warning he slapped him across the face.

In a flash Adam's youthful brawling instincts all came flooding back. He fearlessly lunged forward and spat right in Eduardo's face before quickly throwing his bound fists upward and busting him in the jaw from under his chin, sending the man flying backward. Hector, who was standing at guard behind him, hadn't expected him to make a move like that and tried to grab him, but just as quickly Adam whipped around and used the momentum of his bound hands to swing his elbows back and pound Hector with all his force in the center of his body, leaving him unable to breathe. Right away, he grabbed the knife that had flown out of Hector's hand. Adam then noticed the chain of Emmanuel's pocket watch hanging out of the front of Hector's pants, so he reached down and glared at his captor, then reclaimed his property by snatching it out of the man's pocket.

"I told you I'd get this back," he said. Then he grabbed the flintlock and possibles bag that Hector had placed on a table along the wall.

Santiago capitalized on the moment of chaos and attacked the other guards. He was able to wrestle the knife out of the hand of the man who had been guarding him, and then he slashed the man across his right arm, not dealing him a fatal blow but one that would render him unable to use his dominant hand offensively.

While Drake's leg was hurt, he was not as bad off as he had led everyone to believe, but he was smart enough to stay down until there was an opportunity to fight back. While Santiago dealt with disabling Drake's guard, Adam wasted no time cutting the cords that had bound Drake's hands in front of him.

As soon as his hands were free, Drake delivered a punch to the side of the guard's head that rendered him unconscious.

Eduardo was unarmed and left stunned by the sudden turn of events. He ran towards the door of the hut to call for guards from outside, but Santiago grabbed him and pinned him to the wall by the neck. He said something to him in Spanish, then pressed him even harder against the wall and held a knife to his throat.

Adam shouted, "Wait! Don't kill him! He's your uncle!"

"He's not going to kill him," Drake said. "At least he doesn't want to. He's telling him to call off his guards and let you and your friends go."

"Do it! ¡*Ya!*" Santiago demanded.

Eduardo responded. "¡*Sueltame entonces!*" He looked over at Adam but continued speaking to Santiago. "Let me go, and I will tell them."

Santiago loosened his grip and marched Eduardo out of the hut.

THERE WERE OTHER MEN posted around the compound. They looked to their leader in confusion about what to do, since he was now the hostage. Eduardo called out to them to release the prisoners in the hut. Within moments Martin and Charlie were freed. They quickly ran over to join Adam, Santiago, and Drake.

Then Willis and Jones both appeared on the other side of the compound near the horse pen and were waving their arms.

"Y'all, come on!" shouted Willis. "Let's go!"

He had one horse hooked up to a cart, and Jones was mounted on one of three other horses so that all of them could make a quick getaway.

Adam worriedly looked at his father, who was still holding on to Eduardo to ensure the safety of the others. "What do we do?" he asked him.

"Run! You all go, get out of here! I will deal with him," Santiago said.

"Why don't we bring him with us?" Adam suggested. "There has to be a higher authority than him."

Santiago said, "Not in Havana! Right now there is not!"

Drake spoke: "Your uncle is the law, boy, and everyone falls in line behind him."

"You're joking," said Adam, desperately hoping it wasn't true. He looked at his father.

Santiago just shook his head. Eduardo smiled and raised his eyebrows in a moment of cocky victory, in spite of the fact his nephew was presently holding him at knifepoint.

"What do you want us to do?" Drake asked his old friend.

Santiago thought for a moment, then said something in Spanish. Adam didn't understand, but Drake nodded and motioned for Adam, Martin, and Charlie to just follow him towards where Willis and Jones had the horses.

"What? What did he say?" asked Adam.

"Just come with me," said Drake, hobbling ahead ever faster.

Initially, Adam tried to keep up, calling out behind him, "Tell me what he said!"

Drake kept going and wouldn't answer. "Hurry up!" was his only response.

Adam stopped in his tracks. "I won't take another step unless you tell me what is happening here! Now say something!"

"Your father won't kill him," said Drake as he met Willis and Jones, who had come in their direction with the horses. "Now come on! We have to go!"

"What will happen to him when he lets his uncle go?"

"God only knows," said Drake. At that he pulled himself into a horse cart that was driven by Willis.

Martin and Charlie stopped running halfway between where Adam stood and where Drake, Willis, and Jones were with the horses. They looked back at Adam as though they wanted him to tell them what he wanted them to do.

Santiago could see what was happening, and he yelled at Adam and his friends, "Go! Get out of here! I will be fine, but you are putting everyone in danger the longer you wait around."

Adam wrinkled his brow. "I don't understa— "

"*Just go!*" Santiago demanded.

Adam took a deep breath and one last look at his father, then ran to catch up with the others. Willis drove the horse cart, with Adam and Drake riding along. Martin, Charlie, and Jones all went on horseback. This time Jones led the way, since he knew the terrain better than Drake, Martin, and Charlie. The three of them had not come to the fortress from the northern route along the beach like Adam, Willis, and Jones, but rather had been taken on that long, winding path through the woods, approaching the fortress from the south.

It was impossible for Adam to make sense of what had just happened—not in the last two days, and certainly not in the last two hours. To finally meet his father and then to be ripped away from him just moments later was far too cruel a fate. He could not accept that this was going to be the end. He knew if his father wasn't going to kill Eduardo—and he didn't blame him for not wanting to kill his own uncle—Eduardo would most likely kill him. And Adam couldn't just let that happen.

"Go back!" he suddenly demanded.

Willis turned his head around and looked at him as though he were crazy. "What?" he said.

"I said go back!" Adam attempted to wrestle the reins away from his friend, but Willis held on tight.

"Go back where?" Drake asked. "Back into that death trap? Your father wants you to get out of here *safe*."

"That's just it! My father is back *there*. And he's going to die if we don't go help him! We're armed again and we've got these horses. We can ride back and grab him and bring him with us!"

"You're crazy," said Willis. "Do you know that?"

As soon as he said it, he pulled the reins hard to the left to turn the horses back towards the compound. When Martin and the others realized what was happening, they followed close behind.

As they approached the center of the compound, Adam could see that Santiago was still standing in the same spot, holding Eduardo in order to ensure their safe escape with the horses. When he saw Adam and the others coming back towards him, his eyes grew huge.

"What are you doing?" he yelled. "*¿Están locos?* I told you to leave!"

The horse cart was less than twenty feet away from him now.

Adam called out, "Come on! Just leave him here. They won't catch us. We've got all the horses!"

"I cannot do that," said Santiago. "This will never end if I do not end it today."

"But how? One of you is gonna get killed," Adam replied.

"Maybe, but it will not be my father's brother—not by my hands," Santiago countered. "If it is, this fighting will only continue. I would end up in Hell, and his sons will just come after you."

"Then just leave him!"

At that, Willis rode the cart very close to where Santiago was standing. As they drew near, Adam grabbed the flintlock pistol that he had recovered from the hut and smashed Eduardo in the head with the butt of it, knocking him back.

"Come on!" Adam said to his father.

It took Santiago a moment to reconcile what was happening, but he climbed on the back of the cart quickly, and Willis snapped the reins to start driving them away again.

THE MEN ALL RODE hard and fast across the compound, but Eduardo's men were running behind them, firing their pistols at whatever they could hit. The noise was deafening.

Suddenly, blood splattered inside of the horse cart. Adam quickly looked to see what had happened. His father had been hit. A lead ball had torn through the upper part of his left arm near his shoulder. Santiago howled in pain and shouted something in Spanish that Adam guessed was probably "Oh my God! I've been hit!" Considering Adam was seated on Santiago's left side and they were both leaning on the end of the cart nearest Willis, watching where they were going, it would appear that the bullet was intended for him.

Drake quickly grabbed the pistol that Adam had earlier, and he readied it to fire. He took aim at Hector, who had stumbled out of the hut to help Eduardo, but he missed. He readied the pistol and fired again, but as they were getting farther away and the pistol had unreliable aim, the only thing it accomplished was causing Eduardo's men to fall back. All they had going for them at this point was that the men at the compound had no horses now. They would have to go on foot back to town if they wanted to chase down Adam and the others.

Adam had dealt with a lot of things before, but he had no experience with gunshot wounds, nor did Charlie. Willis knew what had happened, so he looked back and yelled at Adam to tie something around his father's arm to stop the bleeding.

Although it didn't seem like the ball had hit the bone, it

had ripped a huge chunk of flesh when it went into his arm. He was losing blood—and fast. Adam tore off his shirt, then used a knife to cut off one of the sleeves and wrapped it tight around Santiago's upper arm. The wound was massive. The blood was soaking right through the fabric.

"Here." Drake leaned over to assist him. "You're gonna have to get it tight . . . Stop the blood flow, or he could die."

Adam was trying hard not to panic. The cart was bumping terribly as they tore through the woods. As he attempted to cut the other sleeve off of his shirt, Willis took off his belt and handed it to Adam.

"Here," he said. "Fasten this around his arm over that sleeve. Maybe you can get it tight enough to stop the bleeding."

As Drake attempted to hold the sleeve in place, Adam worked quickly to bind it tight with the belt, but the blood was seeping through so quickly that it made his hands slippery, so he was struggling to get the buckle to hold fast. Finally, he was able to get the pin through, and the belt was nice and tight.

As they broke through the Kapok grove to the shore, Adam worried they wouldn't be able to get the cart across the beach. They had to get Santiago back to town and to see a physician, and they had no time to lose. He called out for Willis and the others to stop so he could get Santiago off of the cart and put him on a horse. He determined he would ride with him himself. He could go much faster alone than the group of them could.

The men all worked quickly, and within just a couple of minutes they had hoisted Santiago up onto the horse that Martin had been riding, and Adam climbed up with him and they took off. Drake instructed Jones to ride ahead after Adam, since he seemed to be an experienced horseman. Meanwhile, he and the others continued making their way back towards town as quickly as they could.

When Adam and Jones neared the river, they knew it was too deep to easily get across at the mouth, so they rode south until they could see that the water wasn't very deep and then led the horses across and back towards Havana at breakneck speed.

Santiago passed out along the way, but just before he did he made one request of Adam. "If they cannot help me, please do not stay to watch me die. I want you to remember me as I was alive."

"Hush talking," said Adam. "I'm getting you to the captain. You're gonna be just fine."

He quietly prayed the whole way back to town.

As soon as entered Havana proper, they headed straight for the port and the *Carolina Gypsy*. Adam didn't know any doctors in Havana, but he knew the captain had basic skills to patch up a man with a serious wound.

"Where's the captain?" Adam yelled to Canady, who was down on the docks near the vessel. "Hurry up and go get him!"

Canady ran up the ramp to fetch Captain Phillips.

"Good Lord!" said the captain as he came down the ramp onto the dock. "What's happened here?"

"He's been shot," said Adam, breathless.

"You look awful yourself, son, but I'm glad to see you made it back in one piece."

Adam dismounted the horse but kept a concerned hand on his father until the captain and Canady could help bring him safely down and carry him on board.

Within moments they had laid him on the deck of the ship.

Captain Phillips performed a superficial inspection of the

wound, then said, "This looks ugly. I'm worried that ball may have done more damage to his arm than I can fix. I need to see if I can find a surgeon."

It dawned on Adam that Captain Phillips didn't know yet that Santiago was his father, but nevertheless Adam's face made apparent his intense concern for the man whom Captain Phillips at least knew was one of his rescuers.

"Now listen," the captain told him. "We need to get him moved out of the open and into a nice, quiet place. He can rest in my berth."

"Alright, Cap'n," said Adam.

He, Canady, and the captain all worked together to get Santiago moved into the captain's bunk.

"I'm goin to go into town to see if I can find a doctor to come look at him," said Captain Phillips. "You just make sure nobody moves him under any circumstances. He's lost a lot of blood, and he's obviously gonna need stitches. Right now, though, he can just stay here and rest. I'll be back as quick as I can."

Adam nodded. "Thank you for everything, Cap'n."

Chapter Fifteen

WHEN DRAKE AND the others finally arrived back at the *Gypsy*, Adam wasted no time asking him if someone should go to the Velasquez estate to make whoever was there aware of what had happened.

"His mother, Isabel—your grandmother—she'll need to be informed of what has happened," said Drake. He hesitated, then added, "And she'll want to know about you too, lad."

"She's still alive?" asked Adam, surprised at this revelation.

"Oh, of course. That's what this whole business is about, you know."

Adam wrinkled his brow and shook his head impatiently. "I obviously don't! I didn't even know who my father was until a few hours ago, for goodness' sake!"

"Understood," Drake said. "You didn't understand

everything that was said between your father and Eduardo, I would imagine."

"No, I didn't. I don't speak Spanish, and even when they were talking in English I was lost. That whole thing about him being my father, it kind of had me distracted, so why don't you explain to me what this is really all about?"

Drake scratched his head and shuffled down to sit on one of the steps of the ladder that led to the main deck from the quarterdeck. "Come sit down here. This leg is killing me, and I need to rest my weary old bones. You look like you could use a bit of a rest as well."

Adam reluctantly walked over and took a seat beside him. "Alright. Would you please tell me what you do know?"

"I can't say I'm sure of all the details, but I suppose I've pieced together enough from what I'd already heard from your father over the years, along with that whole bit that I heard the two of them—your father and your uncle, I mean—arguing about today."

"So? What is it?"

"This is how I understand it: your great-uncle is the brother of your grandfather, Juan Diego Velasquez de Castillo."

"Wait a minute," said Adam. "What is this Velasquez de Castillo? I'm fairly certain I remember somebody telling me that Captain Velasquez—my father, I mean—that his name is Velasquez de Leon."

"Right. Well, the way it works is Spaniards take their father's surname, and then their mother's maiden name goes after that. So if you were named with that convention, you'd be Adam Velasquez Fletcher, or Adam Velasquez de Fletcher. Your paternal grandmother's maiden name is Leon, so your father is Santiago

Velasquez de Leon. Eduardo and Juan Diego's mother's maiden name was Castillo, hence the name Velasquez de Castillo."

"Hmph. I understand. Never knew that before."

Drake continued: "Now you've only just learned that Santiago is your dad, of course, so you'd have no way of knowing that the Velasquez family is ridiculously wealthy. Well . . ." Drake took a deep breath before he began to speak again. "Let me clarify. Your father is ridiculously wealthy."

Adam raised his eyebrows. "Why do you say my father?"

"Why? Well, because he is the only son of Juan Diego Velasquez de Castillo, and Juan Diego is the oldest of the two sons in that family—and there were many sisters between them. Naturally, the lion's share of the family's estate went to him and by extension goes to your father for being his only son. When Señor Juan Diego died, he left everything in the possession of his wife—your grandmother, Isabel—during her widowhood to be held for Santiago, and left only a limited, but still enormous, amount to your father. When Señora Isabel dies, *everything* will go to Santiago."

"Yeah, I did hear Eduardo talk about the inheritance, but I don't understand why it had him hell-bent on kidnapping me for ransom, and why it made him ready to kill us today."

"Ah, well, first of all you should understand that your Uncle Eduardo never cared about the ransom. Eduardo admitted as much—that it was only meant to be a distraction. The way I figure it, I think he just wanted to keep you busy and unable to learn who your father was before you got back on this sloop to return to North Carolina. And I'm sure he hoped that your awful experience here would deter you from wanting to ever return."

"So that's what Eduardo meant about how if I had just

stayed his prisoner and everybody went along with the whole ransom thing, I'd already be on my way back home."

Drake nodded. Adam rolled his eyes and turned his head to look away, clearly frustrated.

"Don't feel bad, son. You'd have never met your father if everything went according to Eduardo's plan. And anyhow, I think it's better that it's all come to a head."

"I don't see how it's better," Adam said. "I mean, Eduardo is still angry—not to mention worried—about the estate not going to him. None of that changes. I'm not really sure why he'd have just let me go back to America if that was what he was really planning to do."

Drake tipped his head to the side in assent to what Adam had just said. "That's a good point, but I am seeing a pattern, if you will, with Eduardo. It appears that for some reason—probably just plain old guilt—he doesn't actually want to have to raise his hand to kill anyone in his own family and—"

"But that makes no sense. His whole complaint is that my father isn't legitimately part of his family, that my father's father is not a Velasquez but is some other man."

Drake nodded. "The ravings of a lunatic. I'm not even sure he really believes that. I think he just says that to justify his actions. But regardless of whether he does or doesn't, he knows that Santiago is still for all intents and purposes thought of as a member of that family, and the son of Señor Juan Diego. If he went so far as to kill Santiago or you, it would likely create a moral dilemma of sorts for him."

"Good Lord, man! A moral dilemma? He admitted he tried to kill my mother—with me in her belly!"

"Ah!" Drake raised his finger in a realization. "But think about it. He also said he did not know that she was with child at the time, so in his mind he was probably just thinking of protecting the family's fortune by removing an outside threat."

Adam twisted up his face in disgust. "You say that like you understand him—like it's normal. That man is evil."

"It's most certainly not normal, but being blinded by outrage will only accomplish two things: it will cloud your vision, and it will make you hungry for revenge. The thing is you *should* try to understand the mind of this crazed man, because the fact is he will continue to be a threat to you and your father for as long as he draws breath. By trying to understand him, you may be able to anticipate his next move."

Adam hung his head and looked down between his knees to his brown leather boots. He hadn't noticed it before, but there was blood on them—and also on his dark-tan pants and his cream shirt. It took him back to the moment in the horse cart when his father was shot, blood spattering everywhere. The feelings that came bubbling up from somewhere deep inside told him that what Drake had said was right. And with his history of being impetuous and temperamental, he couldn't afford to let those kinds of feelings take root in his soul. Considering Drake's recommendation that he try to understand Eduardo's mind, he made an observation: "If what you're saying is true, it sounds like he picks and chooses his morality as he sees fit."

"Indeed," Drake agreed.

Adam thought for a moment, then said, "What about Isabel—my grandmother, I mean? Why has he never made an attempt on her life?"

"Hmm . . . That's a fair question. I really have no idea . . . unless it is because he knows that will only lead to Santiago finally receiving his inheritance."

"I get the feeling Eduardo hasn't thought all of this

through. I mean, he may have had some reason for restraining his hand against my father and me in the past, but now . . . Well, now I just don't see what he has to lose by killing both of us."

"You may be right," Drake conceded. "Until just recently he didn't even know you were alive. And maybe his own wishful thinking has stayed his hand all this time."

The two sat in silence for a few moments, both utterly exhausted at the lack of sleep in the last twenty-four hours. Finally, Drake stood to excuse himself. He told Adam he wanted to go home so he could rest and see his wife and baby. He encouraged Adam to try and get some rest as well.

Adam didn't get up, however. Now that he had time to actually sit, he realized he was too tired to even stand. Instead, he just rested his elbows on the quarterdeck behind him and gazed out across the harbor. There were so many ships from diverse parts in nearly every direction all around him. He remembered how excited he had been just a few days earlier when he and his shipmates on the *Gypsy* first spotted Cuba in the distance.

From the time he learned he would be sailing to Havana, and that there may be a man there who might be able to tell him about his father, Adam could hardly contain his excitement. In spite of the fact that the *Gypsy* stopped in a couple of beautiful ports in the Bahamas before finally arriving in Havana, Adam could only think about getting to Cuba, and how his life might change if he could only find Alonso Cordova, the man whose name was scrawled on a piece of paper, the first real hope he'd had for locating his father.

Things went much further than he ever could have imagined, though. Not only did he find out who his father was, he also came face-to-face with him. It felt like a knife in the gut finding him only to be now on the verge of losing him forever.

It occurred to him that while the man who lay there in such a critical state in the captain's quarters might share his blood—and might have even once been his mother's greatest love—he was a complete stranger to him. Sure, they had met once before, but what difference did that make? He would've never guessed that the Spanish captain he'd met the year before was his father.

But when he thought about the little bag of treats Captain Velasquez had given him—the candies and those fireworks that wouldn't explode—it made him smile. Even though the firecrackers might have been duds, they still ended up helping him out of a sticky situation the night he had sneaked into that warehouse. In a way, he thought, it was as though his father wanted to help him even then. Santiago didn't have to give Adam those things. He had done it because he felt compassion for him. He said everyone should go away from his ship with something, so even though Adam had no money to buy anything and tried to pretend he just wasn't interested, Santiago wouldn't take no for an answer, instead opting to fill up one of his little cloth sacks with a variety of goodies free of charge.

Adam knew that he should pray. He wanted to ask God for any little bit of wisdom and guidance that he could give so that he might be able to understand the situation in which he now found himself, but he was too tired to even string his thoughts together coherently enough to pray. He would've spread out right on the stairs where he sat, but they were too uncomfortable. Instead, he went down to the berthing area and found his hammock and collapsed.

Chapter Sixteen

"GET UP, FLETCHER!" Adam was awakened by someone shoving repeatedly on his shoulder. It was Martin. Adam knew without even seeing who it was. He had woken him up in that same way almost every single day that they had been on the *Gypsy*. It was an annoying way to be woken up, considering it caused his berth to swing back and forth.

It took him a minute to collect himself and piece together where he was and all that had happened, and then he turned himself over in his hammock to face Martin. "Is he alright?"

"It's hard to say. I reckon you oughta just come up and see for yourself."

Adam slid out of his berth and went up the ladder to the main deck and then ascended the short ladder up to the quarterdeck.

Just as he approached the door, Captain Phillips came out to speak to Adam.

"How is he?" Adam asked.

"I found a surgeon in town. He's in there with him right now. You'll be able to go in and see him in a minute."

"Is he awake?"

"He is now," said the captain.

Just then a young man, who must have been one of the surgeon's helpers, came out carrying a bowl full of bloody rags. The surgeon was apparently finishing up his surgery on Santiago's arm. Adam tried to look inside, but he couldn't see much, because of the tight quarters.

"I want to thank you for letting Captain Velasquez rest in your berth," Adam said. "It's a good and charitable thing that you've done, sir."

Captain Phillips smiled and wrinkled his brow. "Captain Velasquez? Goodness gracious, boy. You know good and well you don't need to be so formal with me. I've already been told he's your father. Ain't nothin wrong with it if you say so."

Adam nodded. He didn't know if or when he'd ever get used to people acknowledging he had a father, much less knowing who he was. "Yes, sir. Well, all the same I want to thank you for taking him in here, especially when you could've just as easily sent him back to his estate."

"Well, from what I was told," said the captain, "that might've been the most dangerous thing to do—and not just because of his present condition."

"You've heard about that, then?"

The captain gave a bit of a sideways nod. "A little bit."

"Well, I, uh . . ." Adam felt embarrassed. He wondered how much the captain knew, and if it had colored his impression of him to know that his father's family had that kind of conflict within it.

"Don't even give it another thought," said the captain. "Mostly, I'm just happy you're back with us and safe. I'd have two people ready to have my head when we got back to Beaufort if I'da lost you down here."

Adam chuckled.

"While the crew's been tied up with your *rescue* mission," said the captain, "I was able to get some men who work here for Mr. Gomez to help me get those frayed lines repaired. Now we need to head on back home—just as soon as we figure out how to handle this business with your father."

"How do you mean, sir?"

The captain scratched his head and looked like he was thinking about whatever it was he was going to say. "Listen, I'm not sure exactly how to put this, but we've got schedules to keep. We need to get back to Beaufort by the end of the month, and I'm already concerned about the weather we might face on the way back. If we don't make it back in a hurry, it's goin to throw off the whole shippin schedule for the rest of the summer, and it ain't like Emmanuel's goin to want to send out letters to folks sayin, 'Sorry. We might be a little bit late deliverin those things you been waitin on for months.'"

"I see," said Adam. He took a deep breath, unsure of what to say. The captain was right. Between the weather delays on the way to Havana and this whole ordeal with being kidnapped and all, the *Gypsy* was already days behind schedule. Captain Phillips couldn't possibly wait more than another day—two at the most—before setting sail for Beaufort. Adam wondered what that would mean for him and for his father's condition.

He didn't have time to give it too much thought, though.

The surgeon came out of the captain's bedchamber to speak to Adam.

"You are this man's son?" he asked, wiping the last bit of blood off of his hands on a white rag. He had a Spanish accent, but his English was very clear, as if he had spent a good deal of time in British territory.

Adam nodded. "Yes, sir. I'm Adam Fletcher."

"Pleased to meet you." He offered his hand for Adam to shake. "I am Dr. Santos."

"Pleased to meet you as well, sir," Adam said, shaking the surgeon's hand.

"Your father is awake, and he says he wants to see you."

Adam tried to look past him into the cabin where his father lay.

"You are welcome to try and talk to him, of course, but I am not sure how coherent he will be. I gave him some laudanum when I first arrived. It is a medicine that is made with a weak wine that has a little bit of opium in it."

Adam said, "Yes, I have heard of it."

Dr. Santos nodded. "Very good. Well, the laudanum has been helping him with the pain, but it has him in a somewhat euphoric state, so that may make things difficult to have a sensible conversation for very long. Also, he lost quite a lot of blood when he was shot."

"It's just his arm, though," said Adam. "I mean, you stopped the bleeding. He shouldn't die from this, right?"

The surgeon seemed pensive before he answered. "Well, let's just hope he starts to improve and that infection doesn't set in. Amputation is always something we would rather avoid, so his chances are much better if we do not have to go as far as that. What you must understand is that his body has been in shock the last several hours from the blood loss. The lead ball fractured his humerus. That's the arm bone here." Dr. Santos placed his right hand on his left upper arm. "And it grazed his brachial artery. That's the major source of blood flow in the upper arm. I will tell you that it is a miracle that it was not all blown completely apart."

Adam's wrinkled brow and tense stance betrayed his worry. The surgeon could apparently see his concern and seemed as though he wanted to say something to offer him some comfort. "Young man, take heart. The most important thing is that you got him here and your captain was able to find me in a very short amount of time. As great a distance as you were from any sort of immediate surgical assistance, he would never have made it to the ship if his injury had been even a small fraction worse. In fact, even with a master surgeon he would have certainly lost his arm and quite likely would have died."

Adam raised his eyebrows in anxious confusion. "So you're saying as bad off as he is, it could be worse."

"Yes, I suppose it would be reasonable to say that," said the doctor. "As long as he is still alive, he has a chance of survival, although I will not pretend that this will be an easy battle. But of any patient, I always say that if they are alive and not in complete agony, they are most certainly not as bad off as they could be. It is at times such as this that I thank God for opium."

"Has he had anything to eat or drink?"

Dr. Santos shook his head. "No, he wouldn't take anything."

"Should I try to get him to take something?" asked Adam.

"You can certainly try. He needs to drink something at least to keep his organs from drying out, not to mention the laudanum can be binding."

That last bit was more information than Adam needed to

know. He wasn't even sure how to respond, so he just said, "Can I go in to see him now?"

"Of course." The surgeon walked him over to the doorway and said to Santiago, "Your son is here to see you."

As Adam stood in the doorway, he saw Santiago try to lift his fingers to acknowledge what the surgeon had said, but they barely moved.

Adam stepped into the tiny chamber. He wanted to speak, but he didn't know what to say. He wondered how he should address him. Dad? Father? Santiago? Captain Velasquez? *Papá?*

Finally, he just decided to do what came naturally to him. "Hi," he said tentatively as he moved close to his father's bed.

Santiago struggled to turn his head towards his son. "*Ay, mijo,*" he said weakly. He said something in Spanish, and then Adam presumed he repeated himself in English when he said, "Look at you! Such a handsome son I have . . . I am so proud that you are my son."

Adam understood now what Dr. Santos meant about the drug-induced euphoria. He didn't want his father to potentially embarrass himself by talking too much like a drunk would.

"Don't worry," he told him. "You don't have to say anything."

He wondered if he should reach out and touch his father's hand or something, anything to acknowledge some sort of concern, but it felt awkward.

"You do look like me, *mijo,* when I was your age. But maybe you are better looking . . . because of your mother no doubt."

Adam smiled. Even with his shoulder-length, wavy, blackish-brown hair clumped together with sweat and blood and his face washed out and drained of all energy, Santiago still was a handsome man. Adam could imagine how impressive he must've been nearly twenty years earlier.

"Can I get you anything? Would you like something to eat or drink?"

Adam felt helpless as Santiago appeared to struggle to shake his head. "I do not want to eat. I fear I cannot keep food down right now."

"How about a bit of small beer, then?"

Santiago closed his eyes and gave a small nod.

Adam went to fetch some for him. When he came back, Santiago opened his eyes and tried to prop himself up with his good arm.

Adam instinctively leaned over to help him adjust the pillow beneath his head to raise him up. He then assisted his father in holding the mug as he took a few sips of the weak beer before resting it on a small ledge.

"Now," said Santiago, "bring that over here and sit down so you can talk to me." He cocked his head towards a chair positioned under what looked like a table or desk that was built into the wall.

Adam brought the chair over next to the bunk and sat down. "What would you like to talk about?"

"Tell me everything. I want to know everything about you."

Adam chuckled. "That's a lot. Where should I start?"

"What day you were born?"

Such a simple question, and yet it hurt Adam to have to answer it. "The twenty-second of March. I turned eighteen just a few months ago."

"I wish I could have been there," said Santiago. He smiled weakly, but the smile disappeared as quickly as it had come.

"Do you have a sweetheart?"

Adam flashed his brown eyes upward at an angle, and a smile crept across his face.

"You do. I can tell," Santiago teased. "Tell me about her."

"Well, there is a girl . . . but I don't know that she'd consider herself my sweetheart."

"Really? Why not?"

"Hmm . . ." Adam thought about how to explain the situation with Laney Martin. "Well, this girl . . . She's the most beautiful thing I've ever seen, but she's a lady—I mean, she's from a very good family."

"What is wrong with that?"

"Nothing, it's just that I don't have anything to offer her right now." Adam thought for a second, then declared, "But one day I will—at least I hope so."

"But is she kind? Is she virtuous? You should know those are the most important things," said Santiago. "Far above beauty."

"Oh yes, she is both of those," said Adam. Then he remembered something. "You've met her, you know."

Santiago looked confused. "I have met her? When would I have met her?"

"She's Laney Martin. You know her? She's the one who has the dock where you unloaded your cargo last spring—the day we met."

"Ah! That girl?" Santiago raised his eyebrows, pleasantly surprised. "I remember her. She is very beautiful."

"She sure is."

Santiago looked pensive, then said, "Work hard. Learn all that you can from Emmanuel Rogers, or whoever he tasks with training you. You will be then able to make a handsome living and earn this girl's affection." He raised his finger and wagged it at his son. "And then if she does not want to give you her hand, you are better off without her."

Adam nodded and chuckled. "I'll try to remember that."

They were both quiet for a moment as they each tried to think of what to talk about next. Finally, Santiago said, "Have you been a good son to your mother? Are you respectful and obedient?"

Adam pressed his lips together and tried to think of a way to answer the question that would be both truthful and yet not get him into trouble.

"Hmm . . . I guess I'm like anybody. I have my virtues and my vices."

His father raised his eyebrows, indicating that he wanted to hear more about these virtues and vices.

"Well, what I mean is I love my mama. I really do. I've tried to be a good son, but sometimes that's gotten me in trouble."

"How do you mean?"

"Like my apprenticeship with Mr. Rogers. See, I ended up being forced into that because, well . . . I got into a fight with this boy, and Mr. Robins—he's the magistrate—he gave me a choice between jail or an apprenticeship, so naturally I chose the apprenticeship."

"That seems like a very severe punishment for a simple fight between boys."

Adam gave a sheepish smile, knowing he would need to explain further. "Oh, well . . . you see . . . it wasn't really my first fight."

His father gave him a semi-stern face and said, "You fight a lot?"

"Well . . . a little . . . I mean, I used to. I kind of could have a little bit of a quick temper."

"What for? What would you need to fight about so much? This is not what makes you a man."

Oh boy, Adam thought. *This will be interesting.* "I know that. Most of my fights have been defending my mama and her reputation."

Santiago's eyes grew large. "What? Why would you need to do that?"

He really doesn't get it. "You know, because as far as anybody in the town knows, she has been a single mother all this time. Nobody but Valentine knew you two had gotten married, and then you disappeared before I was born. We live in a tavern for goodness' sake. What would you expect people to think?"

His father rubbed at his cheeks and had a concerned look on his face. "I understand."

"Everybody has always just assumed I was a bastard. My mama has never bothered to try to correct anybody, but I have always told them that it wasn't true—that she was married. Of course, she never had your name, though, so . . ."

Santiago pressed his head against the pillow. He looked aggrieved by what Adam had said. "I am so sorry. And this is because I left?"

Adam could tell that his father was being sincere, just as he could see that this aspect of his leaving was something Santiago had never really considered, at least not in any meaningful way.

Adam shrugged. "Well, of course. Folks just thought she was an entertaining girl in the tavern. When I was young as thirteen or fourteen, I was running men out of the tavern who'd come in disrespecting her."

"You are a good son to defend your mother's honor in this way."

Adam didn't say anything. A million thoughts were going through his head, though.

"Tell me why you never came back," said Adam. "I mean, not even to check on us. You never even sent a letter."

Santiago took a deep breath, then motioned for the mug of beer. Adam helped him hold it so he could take a sip.

"We thought we were doing the best thing—the only thing we could to keep you and your mother safe."

"Would you just tell me what happened?"

"It is a very long, sad story."

"I don't care. I think I deserve to know."

Santiago nodded. "You're right. You do." He looked as if he was thinking about how to respond before he started to explain.

Adam listened intently and occasionally asked questions as Santiago told him about what happened the summer of 1747, when the Spanish attacked Beaufort, and how it led him to go back to Havana, never to return to Beaufort to be with his wife and child again. He told Adam how in the August siege there was a fire at the Topsail Tavern and a woman was killed, but it was the wife, or more likely lady friend, of one of the sailors who had taken a room there. She had been drunk and passed out in their room apparently, so she did not know there was a fire and couldn't get out in time. She didn't burn up, but the smoke killed her. Her hair color and build were similar to Mary's, so word had gotten back to Eduardo that Santiago's new bride perished in the fire.

"First of all, how did Eduardo even know about my mother in the first place?"

"That man who kidnapped you—you remember him?"

"How could I forget?"

"His name is Hector Nuñez. He was one of my men a very long time ago. He sailed with me for many years. But at some time my uncle got to him. He paid him money and told him to keep an eye on me as we traveled, and if there was ever any news to report—such as could affect our family's fortune—that he was to come back here to Havana and tell him right away. So that is what he did. Your mother and I were married on my ship. My old friend Alonso performed the ceremony. It was not official to your colony because we did not register it with the court, but in the eyes of God it was as real as it could be. The very next day Hector went missing. We worried something had happened to him, but later we learned that he had gotten passage on one of the vessels from San Augustin that had been sitting off the coast earlier in the summer to go back to Florida, where he then got another vessel to take him back to Havana. There, he told my uncle about my marriage. Apparently, my uncle sent some obscene amount of money to help finance one final attack on Beaufort—the one in August—and that is when the tavern burned."

"Your uncle told them to burn down the tavern?"

Santiago shook his head. "That I do not know. I only know that he was behind the August attack and that he had hoped your mother would perish in it—and when he was told about the woman who died at the tavern, he thought she did."

"You must've known he was behind it then, huh? I mean, why else would you have left and come back to Havana, never to return?"

"Alonso, God rest his soul. Alonso had been warning me for such a long time that he suspected my uncle of doing many terrible things, and that he had heard of awful things my uncle said. He told me many times the man was a snake in the grass, but I did not want to believe him. When I learned that Hector had not just disappeared but that he had gone to tell my uncle about my marriage, and that Hector was one of the men who set fire to the tavern, I—"

"Wait a minute! Hector is the one who tried to kill my mother!?"

Santiago nodded. "He was one of a group of them who tore through the town, burning ships and some buildings on the waterfront, killing livestock, and stealing slaves. Most of the attackers were Negros and mulattos. They had been former slaves from the English colonies who had run to San Augustin for freedom—but they were being led into battle by Spaniards. And thanks to my uncle's money, Hector had become one of the men leading the attack."

Adam was stunned. He didn't know what to say.

"As I was telling you, when I realized that Hector was involved—because Mary had seen him among the men who were setting fire to the tavern—I suddenly came to realize what Alonso had been saying to me all this time was true. Hector had been at my wedding, and now he was trying to burn down the home of my bride."

Adam was incensed. "Why didn't you track him down and beat his ass? Why didn't you kill him?"

His father shook his head. "*Mijo*, your mother had survived, but Hector did not know that. How could I have let Hector know what I knew without giving away the fact that your mother had survived? She was the only one in that tavern who had met him. He never went to that tavern—not like Alonso. And anyway, I will not kill a man in cold blood. If I had caught him in the act myself, I would have done anything I could to save Mary and the others in the tavern, but to go hunt him down and kill him like an animal? That I could not do."

"So that's when you left?"

"Your mother and I, we talked about it. We thought about so many things we could try to do to be together—we even thought about running away to Europe or the Mediterranean to try to start a new life—but my uncle is very well connected the whole world over, and every option would have had us always looking over our shoulders to see if Eduardo or one of his mercenaries was after us." He hung his head and sighed. "*Mijo*, that is no way to live, and that is no way to raise up a child."

"So you just decided to come back to Havana and pretend like she was dead . . . and me?"

Santiago nodded. "That is correct. I came back to Havana, and I grieved horribly. I did not even have to pretend, because I *was* grieving. It was as though she had died to me—and you along with her. I knew I could never make contact with either of you again for fear of my uncle finding out that the two of you still lived."

"You really did stay away to protect us?" Adam was beginning to understand his father's sacrifice all these many years.

Santiago's eyes were welling up, but Adam could see that he would not let himself cry. "Your mother had Valentine and Margaret. They were so good to her—just like her parents—and so they would be like grandparents to you. I knew they would take care of her—and you."

Adam nodded. "They did. They have. Margaret passed away, you know. She died when I was about ten years old."

"I am so sorry to hear that. She was a kind woman. Valentine never approved of my relationship with your mother, because she was only seventeen when we met."

"How old were you, then?"

"I was twenty-three, I think. But Margaret, she did not

mind. She said that she was only fifteen when her father let her marry Valentine, so she did not understand why Valentine thought Mary was too young. Valentine said times change, though."

Adam chuckled. "That sounds like Valentine." He thought for a minute, then had another question. "When did you decide to go back to Beaufort?"

"What do you mean?"

"I mean, you obviously went back occasionally to do business with Emmanuel Rogers. How were you able to do that without your uncle finding out?"

"That was very hard for me," Santiago responded. "But I had to do it. The spring after I had left Beaufort for good, I received a letter from Emmanuel saying that he wanted to do business with me again. I wrote him back and told him that I would come before the summer's end, and I did, but I did not make many trips back to Beaufort—and I always stayed away from the Topsail Tavern. I didn't want it to seem as though I still had any ties there at all, just in case Eduardo had gotten one of my other men to spy on me."

"Did Mr. Rogers know about me? I mean, did he know about you and my mother?"

Santiago looked like he was considering the question before he answered it. "It is possible. The first time I was in Beaufort, he must have known I was spending a lot of time at the Topsail Tavern. And yours is a small town. I am sure he would have known that your mother had a child that next spring. And he may have even realized that it was nine months after I was there, but if he did know about it, he did not say it to me, and we did not discuss it."

Adam realized that it must've been his father that Emmanuel was talking about when he had said that he'd always had his eye on him and was committed to seeing him be successful. At the time he had dismissed the idea of it being his father, since Emmanuel said he had made the promise decades ago, but it was probably just that the old man was trying to be vague about it.

He and his father continued to talk for the better part of an hour before Dr. Santos came back in to give Santiago more medicine.

"He seems to be doing alright now," said Adam. "What's that for?"

The surgeon explained, "I am trying to help him stay ahead of the pain. It is much easier to keep it under control than it is to bring it back down once it becomes intense."

"I see." Adam stood by and watched his father open his mouth to receive the concoction as Dr. Santos administered it from a glass medicine dropper.

"It'll probably make him drowsy, you understand," said the surgeon. "I will be going back to my office now, but your captain knows how to find me. I will be coming back here to check on him first thing in the morning. Until then, do not move him. We do not want to risk further trauma or infection."

Adam nodded. "Yes, sir. I understand."

At that, Dr. Santos excused himself.

"Just sit with me until I fall asleep," Santiago said to Adam.

"I will."

Within moments Santiago had drifted off into a heavy sleep. Adam somehow felt obligated to stay on the *Gypsy* to look after his father, but something was worrying him, and his gut was telling him he needed to find Drake and talk to him. He thought that it would be unlikely that Captain Phillips would let him leave the sloop, given all that had recently happened, but nevertheless he was determined to go, even though he wasn't sure what, if anything, Drake would be able to do.

Chapter Seventeen

ADAM WENT BELOW deck to find Martin. He was right where Adam would've expected him to be. Still, he asked, "Hey, what are you doing?"

Martin, who was with Canady, Willis, and Jones, sitting around a table in the galley playing cards, turned to look at his friend and said, "Tryin to win back my money from these rascals."

"Yeah, right," said Canady. "You just keep right on tryin, fella. The more you try to win it back, the deeper that hole keeps on gettin!"

The other fellows at the table laughed and slapped their knees, but not Martin. He rolled his eyes instead.

"Come with me, then," said Adam.

Martin looked back at the motley crew sitting around that table and appeared to be contemplating his decision for a brief moment before throwing down his cards and bowing out of the game. "I'm done, boys."

"You can always join us later, mate," said Jones. "Maybe you'll win back what all you lost."

Charlie laughed. "I doubt it. His luck don't seem too good these days."

"Right," said Martin dismissively. He patted Adam on the shoulder and urged him towards the tiny staircase and said, "Let's go."

"So where are we going?" asked Martin.

"I need to find Drake. I figure you must know where he lives, since you were with my father before y'all took off looking for me."

"I reckon I do know," said Martin, "but do you really think it's such a good idea to leave the ship right now? I mean, I figure Eduardo and his men are still after you."

"What if they are?" said Adam. "In fact, I'm sure they are, but they will be until either we leave this place or he dies. I just need to find Drake. Are you going to help me or not?"

"Yeah, I'll help you."

Ten minutes later the two of them were venturing down the same narrow street where Martin had gone with Captain Velasquez when they first went to find his English friend.

Martin had to stop for a minute and think about which of the row houses belonged to Drake. They nearly all looked the same, with brightly colored plaster facades and arched entryways.

He noticed a patch of small, warm-colored blossoms of portulaca growing in front of one of the entrances, and he knew that was the one.

"This is it," he said.

Adam stepped forward and gave the door a sturdy knock.

He could hear a baby burst out in tears, then a woman shouting something in Spanish before a half-asleep and shirtless Drake finally came to the door and swung it open. Adam could tell that his father's friend was surprised to see him standing there. It took Drake a second to realize he should invite the boys in.

He stood back and motioned for them to come inside, then called upstairs to his wife. Adam could hear him call out her name, Elena, and then say something in Spanish, but he couldn't understand it.

Drake limped as he showed them into the parlor and invited them to sit. The place was sparsely decorated, though the furniture that the Drakes did have seemed to be of good quality. Some of it was English, and some was Spanish. The exotic ambiance briefly reminded Adam of home—the living quarters back at the warehouse, with Emmanuel's diverse decor from around the world.

"How's your leg?" asked Adam.

Drake grabbed at his injured knee. "My wife bandaged it up for me. Still hurts like hell, though."

He poured himself a shot of rum and offered some to Adam and Martin. Adam declined, but Martin never could refuse a free drink, so Drake poured him some in a glass. "I don't ordinarily drink in the middle of the day, lads," he said, "but it does help to dull the pain." He took a sip, then asked Adam, "How's your father?"

"I think he's doing as well as can be expected," said Adam. "Our captain found a surgeon to patch him up. Apparently, he's lost a lot of blood, and the surgeon has said he'll be keeping an eye out for infection. I got the impression from Dr. Santos that he has a chance to recover from this, but it will be an uphill climb.

He gave him some medicine just before we left. It makes him sleepy."

Drake rested his elbow on his knee and twisted the glass back and forth in his hand, obviously worried for his friend. "I pray he doesn't get an infection. You know what'll happen if he does."

Adam nodded. "Dr. Santos told me—they'd have to amputate."

"Good Lord," exclaimed Martin.

"That's dangerous business, that is," said Drake.

He looked at Adam as though he was wondering if there was some purpose to the visit.

Adam said, "I'm not sure why I even came here, but I thought I should let you know the situation."

"I'm pleased you did, lad, if for no other reason than it shows you care about your father's well-being."

"Has anyone told his mother yet? My grandmother, I mean?"

Drake shook his head. "Not I. I was utterly exhausted when I left our conversation on the ship. I came home straightaway and collapsed in my bed. My sweet wife, Elena, was worried sick about me, so she brought in our baby, and we were all napping upstairs when you knocked on the door just now."

"Well, I'm sorry to have woken y'all," said Adam, "but I didn't know where else to go or who to talk to."

Drake thought for a moment and rubbed his eyes. "Tell you what, let me get cleaned up and dressed, and we'll go over to see your grandmother right now."

The suggestion took Adam by surprise. "Right now?"

Drake stood, drank down what was left in his glass, and

said, "Why not? I've rested up a bit, and there's no good reason to wait. I'd say it's time you met your *abuelita.*"

Adam wrinkled his brow. "What?"

"Your grandmother."

At that, Drake excused himself and went upstairs.

"Oh Lord," Adam said to Martin. "I don't know that I'm ready for this. I wonder what she's like."

Martin clicked his tongue and tilted his head. "I reckon you'll find out."

Within moments Drake came back downstairs and leaned into the room just long enough to say, "Ready, lads?"

Adam gave Martin a worried look and took a deep breath before following Drake out into the street.

"LOOKS LIKE WE'RE ABOUT to get a storm," Drake said as he readied his horse cart. "I'll try to get us there quick."

They were soon on their way towards the Velasquez estate.

As they neared the road along the waterfront, a light rain began to fall. Adam wondered which house was his father's. When Drake finally slowed the cart in front of a massive iron gate between plastered walls, Adam was stunned to see the property that lay beyond. Although it was nearly dusk, he could see that the house was enormous. There was a beautifully manicured lawn and gardens, and two servants were outside with umbrellas, lighting the lanterns that illuminated the lane to the residence.

Drake climbed down out of the cart and rang the bell at the gate. One of the servants looked over at him and called out in Spanish.

Drake responded, "¡*Soy yo, Tomás!*" He then addressed

the servant by name—Felipe—and said something else that prompted the man to immediately recognize him.

"*¡Ay, Señor Drake! ¡Ahorita vengo!*"

Felipe was a tall, slender black man who couldn't have been more than twenty or so. He ran over and opened the gate to let Drake, Adam, and Martin into the property. He explained something to Drake, which Drake promptly translated for Adam and Martin.

"He's just told me that Señor Santiago isn't here, but that Señora Isabel has a visitor." Drake raised his eyebrows at Adam and Martin, indicating his curiosity.

"A visitor?" said Adam. "It couldn't be anything to do with my father."

Drake tipped his head to the side. "We'll find out."

He said something else to Felipe, who then motioned for them to bring the horse cart up near the main house so they could leave it under a shelter out of the rain.

As soon as they had done that, Felipe led them both to the main house and invited them into the foyer. As the three of them stood there, Drake explained that another servant would soon come and show them to the salon where she was receiving her visitor. They needed to be announced first, though.

As they waited for the other servant, they heard a crack of thunder outside, and the rain began to fall much heavier. They could hear it beating against the windows as the wind drove it towards the house, and they were grateful to have made it indoors just in time.

Adam had never been in a house so enormous before, nor had he seen such fine furnishings. In fact, la hacienda Velasquez made even the most prominent Beaufort citizens look like paupers.

Martin had already seen the palatial residence, so while he was still impressed, he was able to contain himself. He whispered to Adam, "Close your mouth! You look like some country bumpkin!"

Drake must've overheard what Martin said because he chuckled. Adam shot an annoyed glance at Martin but closed his mouth nevertheless and made every effort to act natural.

Another servant could be heard walking on the marble hallway that went behind the grand staircase in the foyer into another part of the house. They soon saw him appear from behind the staircase, and he instructed that they should follow him.

They walked through an ornate, arched entryway that was decorated with tiny, brilliant mosaic tiles and were then led down a long hallway that had at least four large rooms connected to it, but all of the doors were shut. At the end of the hallway was another mosaic-tiled entryway, beyond which was a little alcove where drinks could be prepared and presumably served to guests in the room beyond. Then there was a heavy oak pocket door, which the servant knocked upon twice quickly before sliding it open and leading the three men inside.

Señora Isabel was seated directly across from the entryway of a great room. She wore a dress that was a muted amethyst shade with intricate black embroidery and black lace as trim. Her black hair was pulled tightly back into some kind of braid that was twisted up into a knot, and draped over her head she wore a delicate black lace veil. It did not cover her face but looked as though it was pinned somehow into her braid. Adam figured it was probably typical apparel for a widow, albeit a very wealthy widow.

She only had a few strands of gray hair that Adam could see. It was surprising to him that her hair was as dark as it was, considering her age. In Beaufort, older ladies almost always had hair that had either gone completely gray or white.

The room had a domed ceiling that was cream-colored plaster with gilded beams. The walls were painted a wine red, and the furnishings all had either dark wood or gilded frames. The cushions around the room were made of silk and covered in various jewel tones. There were a few detailed Oriental rugs around the floor of the room—one very large one right in the center, then a couple of long ones that went along the sides, and a third long one that went across the back side and was just in front of where a wall made almost entirely of huge windows and two sets of double doors was.

Señora Isabel's guest was seated across from her but with his back towards Adam, Drake, and Martin.

The servant announced them, and Drake began to address Señora Isabel in Spanish.

Before he could even finish speaking, she said in English, "Tomás, I was just learning about the events that transpired this morning."

At that her guest whipped around in his chair and looked back at Drake, Adam, and Martin. It was Eduardo. His jaw was bruised, and his bottom lip had a dried cut and was swollen from where he'd accidentally bitten it when Adam busted him in the face back at the fortress. In a very calm voice he said something to Isabel in Spanish and glanced between her and Drake, then tipped his head in the direction of Adam and looked again squarely at Drake.

"You rotten bastard!" Drake said in a low voice.

He looked like he was about to dive across the room and attack him when Señora Isabel called out, "¡Basta! ¡Basta! What kind of madness is this?"

She rang a little bell, and within seconds two very muscular servants burst into the room ready to impose calm on the situation.

Adam's heart was about to pound right out of his chest. Why was Eduardo here? What had he been talking to Isabel about? And what did he say that so infuriated Drake?

"This is him, Tomás?" Señora Isabel stood from her chair and angrily motioned at Adam. "Why would you bring an imposter, a *thief*, into my home? What are you thinking?"

Eduardo smiled as he observed the confusion.

"Imposter?" said Drake. He stepped beside Adam and put his hands on each of his shoulders and gently nudged him towards Isabel. "This is your grandson! This is Santiago's son! Look at him, for heaven's sake!" He took some strands of Adam's hair that had fallen out of his ponytail down the sides of his face and tucked them back behind his ear so that the old woman could see the boy's face better, then turned and pointed at Eduardo. "That lying snake wanted to kill him, and now your son is fighting for his very life because one of Eduardo's men shot him!"

At that, Eduardo stood and spoke to Isabel but kept his eyes locked on Adam. "I would have never shot the son of my dear brother. My officer was only trying to stop that imposter from riding away with your son, but he missed and hit Santiago instead."

"This is madness!" said Isabel. "Why would my son have been riding away with you, whoever you are?" she said to Adam.

"Because he was trying to kill us," Adam responded, pointing at Eduardo. "First, he hired some men to kidnap me, but I escaped. He had sent a—"

"Wait! Just wait!" said Isabel. "Slow down. Please. I

understand English very well, but I cannot follow what you are saying if you are speaking this fast."

She sat back down in her chair and waited for Adam to continue.

Eduardo said something to her frantically in Spanish, to which she responded, "You be quiet. I have listened to all that you have said, and I will hear what this boy says." She nodded in Adam's direction, then said, "Before you tell me what you claim happened, please tell me who you are and why you are here in Havana."

Adam took a deep breath. His heart was pounding, and the words he wanted to say were flying through his brain. He would have to make a real effort to speak slowly for her, though.

"My name is Adam Fletcher. I am an apprentice to a shipping merchant. My master is a man named Emmanuel Rogers, of Beaufort, North Carolina, and I came to Havana on his ship, the *Carolina Gypsy*. I have never been on a trade expedition to the West Indies before, but my master wanted me to learn about coopering on the ship." He paused for a moment, then said, "Did you understand all of that so far, ma'am?"

Isabel nodded. "Yes. You may continue."

"I grew up with only my mother, but I was told before I came on this voyage that my father left for Havana before I was born but never returned. I was also told that there was a man here who might be able to tell me something about my father."

"Who was this man?" asked Isabel.

"His name was Alonso Cordova."

Adam could see that Isabel's eyes were beginning to water. He recognized that same steely face his mother sometimes made when she was trying hard not to cry. All she said was, "Please go on."

"After we unloaded the *Gypsy* and got her reloaded with cargo for the return journey, our captain gave us shore leave. That first night in port we all went out, and then the next morning I was going to go with my friend Martin here to try to find Mr. Cordova. The thing is, Martin was late, and he didn't meet me on time, so I decided to go by myself. I went to that plaza and was asking around—"

"Wait, slow down, please. You are talking very fast again. What is that last thing you said?" asked Isabel.

"I was saying that I went to the plaza—that marketplace— and asked around for someone who might be able to help me translate, so I could try to find Mr. Cordova. A man ended up approaching me—a man I later found out used to work for my father, but now he works for him." He pointed at Eduardo. "His name was Hector. He offered to help me and said he knew the family of the man I was looking for and that he would take me to them."

"And you went with him?" asked Isabel.

Adam nodded.

She and Eduardo exchanged some terse words in Spanish, but Drake translated so that Adam knew what they were saying. Drake said, "She just asked Eduardo if what you were saying was true. He admitted that the man who went over to help you worked for him, but he explained that he had already figured you were an imposter and that you were only claiming to be Santiago's son so that you could try to claim a piece of the family's fortune."

"No!" shouted Adam. "That doesn't even make any sense! I only learned a few hours ago that your son was my father. I only had the name of Alonso Cordova!"

Eduardo laughed and said, "He is lying."

Isabel wrinkled her brow, then asked Eduardo, "How

would you have known he was trying to claim to be Santiago's son?"

"Dear Isabel, I am *alguacil mayor*. You already know I have men all over the place." He looked around the room, waving his hands, and said, "Even the walls have ears."

Still looking confused and concerned, Isabel said to Adam, "Have you never known anything about the identity of your father?"

Adam shook his head. "No. My mother never would tell me anything about him other than that he was a sailor and had come to Beaufort the first time in late 1746. She said they fell in love, and by late that next spring they were married on his ship. She was only seventeen, and her guardian would not allow her to marry him, so they married in secret. My father had business to tend to in other ports—at least that's what she told me—so he left, but then he never came back."

"And when were you born?" asked Isabel.

"I was born on the twenty-second of March in 1748."

"Who told you the name of the man—Alonso Cordova—before you came here to Havana?"

"Valentine told me," said Adam. "Valentine Hodges. He's like my grandfather. He was my mother's guardian after she was orphaned as a young girl, and he owns the Topsail Tavern, which is where I was born and was raised by my mother."

"How are you a—how do you say?—*aprendiz* of this man you said?"

"Apprentice? You mean Emmanuel Rogers?" Adam asked. "Yes."

"I was bound to him in May of last year."

"He is not the one who told you of this first mate?" Isabel asked.

Adam shook his head. "No, I said it was Valentine who told me."

Eduardo interrupted again and said something to Isabel in Spanish. Drake interrupted him, and there was a heated exchange.

"Damnit!" Drake exclaimed. "Everyone in this room"— he motioned to the guards— "except maybe those two speaks English! Why leave this boy out of the conversation? And let's not forget while we're all here arguing: your man *shot* Santiago!"

"He is being brought here as we speak," said Isabel. "I have arranged for it."

Drake, Adam, and Martin all looked at her, completely stunned at this revelation.

"You can't move him!" said Adam. "He's lost a lot of blood, and he's already really bad off. The surgeon said he really shouldn't be moved, and he's worried about an infection starting."

Isabel nodded. "I understand that, which is why I sent my personal physician and four of my servants in my coach to go to this ship of yours and bring him here. Once we have him in his bed, he will not need to move again until he is recovered completely. He will rest much more soundly in his own bed with our servants taking care of his every need. Also, this home is, I am sure, much cleaner than your ship. It will be healthier surroundings for him to convalesce."

"Respectfully, señora," said Adam, "you shouldn't do this yet. It might be too hard on him to be moved right now. It could kill him. Not to mention I don't trust that man"—he pointed at Eduardo—"and he may even have someone finish the job that they started earlier today. It'll be a miracle if my father makes it here from the *Gypsy* alive!"

"This boy is a liar," insisted Eduardo. "He is simply a liar."

Isabel ignored his comment. She directed her response to Adam. "Do not be absurd, boy! I will not leave my son to die on some strange ship."

"You'd rather him die here, then?"

"*Con la ayuda de Dios* he will not die, but to answer your question, if he were to die God forbid, yes, I would rather it be here in our home."

"Are we forgetting that this man—*this criminal* who *you* have invited right into your home—he is to blame for all of this?" Drake said, pointing again at Eduardo.

"*No!*" Eduardo fumed. "The only criminal in *this* room is that boy, and I will not sit by as he comes into my country and tries to take what is rightfully mine!"

For a couple of seconds no one said anything.

Finally, Isabel spoke. "What is rightfully yours, Eduardo? You mean what is rightfully my son's?"

Eduardo inhaled sharply and let out a fast sigh. "Of course that is what I mean. You know I am not so good with the English as you. I meant what rightfully belongs to the Velasquez family."

"Why don't we tell Señora Isabel about how *you* are the reason Santiago never went back to his boy?" Drake said to Eduardo. "Let's just have this out here right now."

Eduardo looked at him in confusion, and then he suddenly appeared to be nervous.

"What is this?" Isabel inquired.

Drake rubbed his chin and looked like he was contemplating what he would say. He walked over to where Isabel was and took a seat on the end of the chaise lounge next to her chair.

"Señora Isabel, your son and I, we've been friends for many years now, right?"

Isabel nodded. "*Sí, claro.*"

"We're like brothers, Santiago and me, and we've shared a lot of stories about our pasts." He went on to give her a brief history of what he knew about Santiago—and Mary and Adam—along with how it was because of Eduardo that Santiago never returned to his wife and child. He never did tell Isabel that Eduardo had questioned Santiago's legitimacy, though.

Isabel wrinkled her brow. "Is this true?"

"It is all lies, but that is what liars do. *They lie*," said Eduardo.

"I swear it's the truth," said Drake. "I'm telling you that man"—he pointed at Eduardo— "is a snake in the grass. He was making all kinds of accusations back at that fortress he has in the woods, and threats about how he was not going to let Santiago or his son take the Velasquez family inheritance away from his sons."

"I said I was not going to let this imposter come in and take our family's inheritance," Eduardo insisted to Isabel.

"Your sons would not inherit any of Santiago's property unless he dies without heirs," said Isabel. "If this boy is telling the truth—if he is the child of my son—then Santiago has an heir. Is that why you kidnapped this boy?"

"I am telling you, Isabel, he is lying! He is not Santiago's child! He is a stupid English boy who is trying to come in to Havana and steal the family's fortune!"

"That would make no sense if he did not know that Santiago was his father," she commented.

"That's just it! I didn't know," said Adam, "and for what it's worth, I'm not interested in any inheritance. I only wanted to know who my father was. That's all I ever wanted when I came here."

"What were you planning to do with him, Eduardo?" asked Isabel.

Eduardo shrugged, then said, "I wanted only to scare him so that he would leave and not come back with his lies."

"You say you did not know my son was your father, as you claim," Isabel said to Adam. "So I am wondering how he came to be involved with this business."

Martin stepped forward. "Excuse me, but I can explain that, ma'am."

Isabel gave them all a confused look, then nodded. "Fine. I am listening."

"When I realized Adam had taken off without me to look for this Cordova fella, another shipmate, Charlie, and I went and told our captain—he's Charlie's big brother, by the way—that Adam had gone off somewhere, but that we didn't know where he was. We waited for him for a right good long while, but he never showed up, so we finally knew we had to tell our captain. He told us we should go look for Captain Velasquez, since he is a friend of our boss, Emmanuel."

He looked at Isabel to try to ascertain whether she had understood all of what he had just said.

She nodded and said, "Yes, continue."

"I came here to this very house with Charlie just a couple of days ago, and your servants let us in. We were able to talk to your son. We didn't know he had any connection to Adam at all. We only knew that he lives here and that he speaks Spanish, and that he might be able to help us find our friend."

"So what happened?" asked Isabel.

"Well, it's kind of funny, but by the time we figured out where Adam had been taken, he'd already escaped. And then what do ya know? He was coming to look for us! We had been put in this little prison hut over at that fortress he has." He motioned at

Eduardo, then looked back at her to make sure she understood everything.

"All of you? How are you free now?" she asked.

"That man there"—he pointed at Eduardo—"didn't lock Captain Velasquez in there with us. He wanted to see him privately. But as for how we came to be freed, all I can say is that your grandson has enormous . . ." He stopped himself midsentence, then smiled meekly and said, "Well, he's very courageous, ma'am. Soon as he learned we'd gone off looking for him, he got a couple of other fellas from our ship to go with him back to that snake pit. To make a long story short, Adam and your son—together—demanded that he let us go so that we could escape."

Eduardo said nothing. He just leaned back in his chair with one leg crossed over another and stared blankly ahead with a disgusted look on his face.

Isabel seemed to take note of his lack of reaction and asked him, "Eduardo, tell me something."

The man slowly looked up and met her gaze. "¿*Qué?*"

"If this young man and others were with your nephew, what cause did you have for arresting them?"

Eduardo's face turned red in fury. He leaned forward, then began ranting to Isabel in Spanish.

Drake translated as quickly as he spoke. "He says that compound we wandered into is a secret defensive base in case there's ever another attack on Havana like the one back in '62. And he says, how was he to know that we weren't criminals or some kind of threat? He claims when he saw that Santiago was with us, he locked us up so that he could get Santiago alone in case he was being held under duress."

Martin let out a loud laugh. "Good Lord Almighty!

There's a special place in Hell for men who can lie as good as you do, Eddie!"

"How dare you!" Eduardo fumed. "You will not speak to me that way!"

"Well, I reckon I just did," said Martin matter-of-factly.

Eduardo sprang from his chair and flew across the room. The guards weren't able to move quickly enough to stop him from lunging at Martin, but Martin responded quickly and swerved out of the way, then grabbed Eduardo and pulled his arm up behind his back and held him like that until he winced.

"That is enough! This violence must stop *now!*" demanded Isabel.

Martin let Eduardo go but gave him a bit of a push. Thrown off balance, Eduardo started to fall and was only able to steady himself by grabbing hold of a gilded table, knocking several fancy-looking objects, including a porcelain statue, off of the marble top and onto the floor.

Isabel motioned for her guards to grab both Martin and Eduardo and separate them.

"I apologize for all of this confusion, señora," said Drake, "but we have stood here and listened to your brother-in-law tell lie upon lie, and after all we have been through, and your son's present condition, our patience has worn a little bit thin."

"I do not know who to believe," said Isabel. She looked at Eduardo with some disgust and said, "Eduardo and I have never been very close, but I do not know this boy at all. They will be here with my son soon. I pray that he can help me to make sense of what has happened."

"Ma'am," said Adam, "I pray that he can too, but regardless, I want you to know that I had no idea of the mess I'd stir up by just trying to learn something about my father. The fact is if he'd have been able to be around to raise me like a father should, I reckon none of this would've happened in the first place."

Isabel was left speechless.

Adam ran his fingers back through his hair and thought for a moment. He still had one more thing to say. His dark-brown eyes met hers in an intense gaze. "I am glad I met my father, but I realize you don't know me, and your own brother-in-law acts like he's going to do whatever it takes to get me out of the picture. But the truth is there really would've been no need for any of this—for me to have been kidnapped, or for your son, my father, to have been shot. If I had only known he had been alive and well and living here in Cuba this whole time, I don't even know that I'd have bothered to try to meet him. I sure don't want a piece of anything that's here. I just want to go home. In fact, I'm leaving now, and you don't have to worry about me coming back again uninvited."

At that he turned and walked out of the room, straight down the hall, and went out of the house into the storm.

ADAM DIDN'T EVEN BOTHER to shield his head from the rain as he crossed the lawn towards the lane that led out to the gate.

Soon Martin ran out after him and shouted, "Wait for me, damnit!"

Adam turned and strained to look back at his friend, who was running to catch up. "Hurry up, then. I want to get off of this estate and get back to the *Gypsy*."

Martin nearly slipped on the cobblestone drive before he caught up with Adam. He grabbed his shoulder. "But your father . . . They should be back here with him any time now. Don't you want to see how he fared on the trip over?"

Adam shook his head and pulled away. "No, I really don't. There's not a damned thing I can do for him, anyway. His mother seems determined to have things her way, whether she kills him in the process or not. This whole family is crazy, and I'm sorry I ever went looking for him."

He started walking fast again.

Martin ran to catch up and talked as he walked alongside him. "You can't mean that. I mean, that uncle of yours, he's out of his mind."

Adam scoffed. "You think so, huh? Why do you think I'm ready to leave this place?"

He walked briskly until he got to the gate, then unlocked it and pushed it open. He thought for a second about how to lock it back from the outside but then decided not to worry about it.

"You can't run from him. He'll come after you, you know." Martin was nearly having to yell now the rain was so loud.

"I know," Adam shouted, "and when he does I'll be ready for him. My father may not have been able to bring himself to deal with the threat all those years ago, but I'm sure not going to let him keep me looking over *my* shoulder for the rest of my life."

Just as suddenly as it had began, the rain begin to lighten up, much to their relief.

"And then what, Adam? What about his sons? You don't think they'll be after you too if you do somethin to their daddy?"

Adam shrugged and continued walking. He reached back behind his head and twisted his short ponytail to squeeze out the excess water. "Maybe they will, but I reckon I'll just have to cross that bridge when I get to it."

Martin shook his head. He looked as if he was searching for the right words to say to his friend. "You know," he said, "it's probably a good thing that he didn't stick around Beaufort, anyway."

Adam looked at Martin like he was crazy.

"I'm not jokin. I can't see how it would've made things easier for you growin up with a Spanish surname after the summer of '47. I mean, think about it—Adam Velasquez?" He chuckled. "That don't even sound right."

Adam looked at his friend in disbelief, then fought the urge to grin in amusement. "You're out of your mind. You know that, right?"

"Maybe so," Martin insisted. "But I still don't think you ought to be so hasty that you run on out of here without even botherin to find out what happened with your father. I'm tellin you, you'll regret it if you do. It ain't like we live right down the road. You can't just run back to check on him if you change your mind."

"I realize that, I do, but I can't stop thinking about the fact that if I'd have just left things alone, none of this would've happened. And it isn't like there's a thing in the world I can do to make any of this any better." He looked at Martin and wondered whether or not his friend would argue with him about that. When he didn't, Adam continued: "Now I just want to get as far away from this godforsaken island as I can and never come back. The way I see it is this: my father told me that he didn't want me to watch him die. He wanted me to remember him when he was alive. If he dies, I'm honoring his wishes by going on back to Beaufort. If he doesn't die, then it will be up to him whether he's going to come see me in Beaufort now that the cat's out of the bag."

"So this is really it? You're just goin to go back and tell the captain you're ready for us to leave? Because you know he'll give you another day or so if you need it to tie up loose ends."

"Yes, this really is it."

"I'd never have figured you'd quit so easily." Martin stopped in the street. "You're just gonna turn tail and give him exactly what he wants."

Adam stopped for a second, but he didn't look back. He hung his head and clicked his teeth in frustration, then started walking again. Martin caught up again, but they went the rest of the way back to the *Gypsy* in silence.

Chapter Eighteen

WHEN ADAM AND Martin boarded the *Gypsy*, they couldn't tell if their shipmates were resting down below because of the rain or if they were out in town. They did see that Captain Phillips was around, however, thanks to the soft glow of a lantern that illuminated the windowpanes of his cabin.

"I'm gonna go talk to him," said Adam.

"Alright. I'm gonna go get some sleep myself," said Martin. He disappeared down the ladder that went below deck.

Adam knocked on the door.

The loud voice inside said, "Come on in."

Adam let himself in and saw the captain sitting at the built-in desk, writing in his log book.

"I guess they took him, huh?" Adam observed.

The captain nodded, then turned around and invited

Adam to pull out a chair from his small dining table and take a seat. Adam sat down and rested his elbows on the table and his head on his palms, but he didn't know what to say.

"Men showed up here not long after you left. Said they were here to pick him up and carry him home," said the captain. "I tried to stop them, but Captain Velasquez said it was alright, that he knew them." He hesitated for a minute, then said, "I've gotta tell you, it was a little bit of a surprise. I wouldn't figure anyone else could've already known about what had happened to come get him so quick."

"Oh. Well, I can answer that for you," said Adam. "It was the same man who had me kidnapped, and the same man who's at fault for him being shot to begin with—his uncle."

The captain twisted up his face. "Drime! His own uncle!"

"It's the truth! I wish I were joking."

"What in the world happened?"

Adam proceeded to explain to the captain how he and Martin had gone to find Drake, and the three of them ended up going over to the Velasquez estate, only to find Eduardo was already there and talking to his grandmother. Then he told him about how Martin had nearly gotten into a fight with Eduardo, and about how he ended up getting frustrated with the whole situation, so he left and came back to the ship.

"Sounds like a right fine mess if you ask me," said the captain. "I don't blame you for stormin out, but I think you're gonna have to go back again and see him at least one last time before we leave just so your spirit will be at peace when we go home. You don't even know right now how he's doin. He might've taken a turn for the worse with them moving him like they did."

Adam untied the cord that was holding his ponytail and ran his fingers back through his hair and massaged at his scalp in an effort to ease his aching head. "I know. That's one thing I'm afraid of."

"Whatcha afraid for? I reckon if it were my dad, I'd wanna see him no matter what, but especially if he was really bad off. I'd hate for him to die and me not be able to see him one last time."

"I understand that"—Adam leaned his elbows on the table again—"but my father told me he didn't want me to see him die. His exact words were, 'I want you to remember me as I was alive.' And I want to honor that."

"So that's why you don't want to go back?"

Adam gave the captain a puzzled look.

"I mean, you sure you ain't just usin that as some kind of excuse to not have to go back and possibly face Eduardo again, or even your grandmother? Or maybe you don't think you can handle watchin your father die."

Adam straightened his back and bristled at the captain's comments. "Are you trying to say I'm some kind of coward?"

"Whoa! Settle down, boy. I didn't say that. I'm just sayin that maybe you're just havin second thoughts about diggin into all this mess from the past."

"Of course I'm having second thoughts about digging into all this mess from the past, but it's too late to change that now. I've got a father who's been shot, a grandmother who doesn't even know who I am, an uncle who tried to kill me, and a mother who never wanted me to come here in the first place! And now I have to wonder if that demented man is going to follow me back to Beaufort, bringing all these problems with him."

The captain clicked his tongue and looked down. "Yeah, I can surely understand why you'd be concerned. I wish I knew what to tell you, but the only thing I know is that if you don't go back and at least leave things in a good way with your grandmother—and find out your father's condition—you'll regret it later. It'll eat you up inside."

Adam thought for a minute, saying nothing. He took a deep breath, then let out a sigh. "You're probably right." He stood up as if he was about to excuse himself, then said, "I just need to think about everything for a little while . . . figure out the best way to handle this. I know this much, though: if Eduardo comes after me again, I may just kill him myself."

Adam didn't give the captain a chance to respond. He just turned and went right out of the cabin and down to his berth to get some sleep.

"¡SEÑOR ADAM! ¡SEÑOR ADAM! ¡*Despierta!*"

Adam turned over in his hammock and rubbed his eyes. He was surprised to see two men from the Velasquez estate standing there beside his berth, trying to wake him in a hurried whisper.

"What is it?" he asked.

In a very thick Spanish accent, the taller man said, "Your presence is required at the hacienda Velasquez. Señora Isabel has sent us this night to bring you there to her."

Adam wrinkled his brow. It took him a moment to make sense of what they were telling him.

"What?" he said. "I'm not going there now. You must think I'm crazy."

"Señor Adam," said the shorter man, "you must. La señora has told us not to come back unless we bring you with us."

"How did you find me?" asked Adam.

The shorter man said, "It is good you are having these *cajitas* with your names on the top of them. This is how we know you was in this *hamaca*."

Adam looked around the berthing area. From what he could tell, Willis and Canady were also down there and sleeping, but he wondered where Martin, Charlie, and Jones were. "How'd you even get on the ship?" he asked.

"There is no one up the stairs," said the taller man.

Adam gave him a surprised look. "No one? There's always somebody up there."

"Maybe it is because it is raining—very bad outside—and it is very late. Maybe the others are out enjoying a nice time in the town."

It made sense. Now that Adam was on board and Santiago had been moved back to his estate, they had to know the *Gypsy* would be leaving soon. The men would want to spend every bit of free time they had enjoying their shore leave. As his still-sleepy mind started to clear a bit, he asked, "What does she want with me? Is my father alright?"

The shorter man gave a doubtful smile and cocked his head and said, "We do not know his condition, but it is very important that you come there with us right now."

"Is Eduardo there?" Adam wanted to know.

Shorty said, "Do not worry yourself, Señor Adam. He was sent away this night by la señora, but she want to talk to you now. Please! Let us hurry!"

"How do I know I can trust any of what you are saying, that I'll be safe?"

"You will just have to trust us," said Shorty.

"Please," said the tall one, "I will tell you I swear on my life you are in no danger with us. The señora has no intentions to harm you in any way, I assure you."

Shorty nodded in agreement. "Yes. He is telling the truth to you."

They both looked at Adam, waiting for an answer.

His brain was telling him he'd be crazy to trust anything that anybody from the Velasquez estate said, but in his gut he believed the two men.

He slowly slid out of his hammock and was about to go with them when the tall man said, "If it will make you feel more safe, please bring one of your friends with you. It is alright if you do it."

Adam considered his offer for a second, then shook his head and said, "No, I don't need to bring anybody else into this at this hour. Let's just go."

Chapter Nineteen

WHEN ADAM WAS escorted back into the Velasquez home, he was taken to where Isabel was waiting for him in the family's chapel. As he stood at the entrance, he observed that it was a small room with three ornately carved pews with red velvet cushions. His grandmother was sitting in the front row. In the front of the room was an altar, something Adam had heard about but never actually seen. There were some candles burning, and the centerpiece was a tall crucifix that looked like it was crafted from mahogany—which Adam was beginning to realize was a very popular wood in Cuba. To the right was a bowl, which he assumed was a font of holy water. In the center were two books. The first said "Santa Biblia," so he guessed it was the Bible, and the other was a smaller book, but he could not read any title on it. To the left of the crucifix was a globe-shaped object made of bronze with smoke coming out through the carved designs around the top, and behind that a statuette of the Virgin Mary. As he stepped farther into the room, he could smell that it was fragrant, so he assumed the smoke must be incense. There were some other small objects on the table that he could not identify, but it was of no concern to him. The only thing he wanted to know was why he had been brought here.

Adam was unsure of whether he should quietly take a seat and wait for her to address him, or if he should say something first.

When Isabel heard him come in, she turned and looked at him. "Thank you for coming," she said. "Please, come sit down here." She motioned to a place beside her on the pew.

Adam tentatively stepped forward and sat down beside her.

"What is this place?" he asked.

"This? This is like our family's church." Isabel kept her eyes fixed on the altar ahead and smiled gently as she rubbed the beads of what looked like a long necklace between her fingers.

"You have your own church? You don't go to a real church?" he asked, perplexed.

"Of course we attend *la misa* at the cathedral, but this is our altar. We are a Catholic family. This is where we come to pray and meditate and to say our *credos* and *el rosario*."

"You have to come here to pray?" Adam asked. "Why can't you just pray anywhere?"

"Of course we can pray anywhere, but I feel closer to God here. This is a special place for us. And Nuestra Señora intercedes for us here." She nodded her head forward, indicating the statue of Mary.

Adam was confused by the concept, but he wasn't going to spend time asking her to explain any further. He felt certain a discussion of the differences between Protestantism and Catholicism was not why she had sent for him.

"How's my father?" he asked.

Isabel looked at her hands as she continued to move the rosary beads between her fingers. "It is so strange to hear you say that about my son, for you to call him 'father.'"

Adam didn't respond.

"He spoke to me," she said. "When they brought him here . . . Just for a few moments he was conscious and—"

Adam interrupted her. "Wait! He was only conscious for a few moments?" He felt mild panic. "Did something happen? Is he already . . . ?"

Isabel leaned her head towards Adam, with the slightest smile on her face, and said, "He is sleeping very soundly. The medicine they are giving him—it is very strong, yes?"

Adam nodded. "Oh, well, I reckon it is."

"I was saying to you, when he was awake for a few moments he told me what I already knew."

"What's that?"

"That you are his son."

"You already knew?" Adam asked, incredulous. "You sure didn't act like you already knew when I was here earlier today."

"I knew. I didn't want to believe it, but I knew." She turned and looked at him and smiled. "I can see it here, around the eyes." She motioned to her own eyes, apparently uncomfortable or unwilling to brush her fingers against his face. "And that hair you have." She admired his appearance. "I bet it curls up just a little bit when it is shorter or even when it is wet, does it not?"

Adam reached up and grabbed some of his hair in his palm and said, "Yeah, I reckon it does."

"Do you know how you call me? In Spanish, I mean?" she asked.

Adam shrugged. "Señora Isabel?" He shook his head, unsure of what she meant.

"I am your *abuela*—Abuela Isabel."

"*Abuela* means grandmother," he mused. "Hmph. I've never had a grandmother, or a grandfather. Both of my mother's parents died when she was a girl. I only ever had Valentine. He's kind of like a grandfather—like I was telling you earlier today."

There was silence between them for a moment.

"And of course I never knew anything about my father, so I couldn't have known you or his father." He was thoughtful for a moment, then asked, "How do you say 'grandfather'?"

"*Abuelo.*"

"*Abuelo. Abuela.*" Adam repeated the words one more time before asking, "My *abuelo* died sometime back?"

Isabel looked down again and nodded. "Yes. My husband died several years ago. He was so good to Santiago. He was a wonderful father."

There was more silence. Adam felt awkward. While he was glad to know she at least was willing to acknowledge who he was, he wondered if this was why she had sent for him—just to let him know that she believed him. Or was there something else?

It occurred to him that she had never answered the question he asked earlier. "Well, how is he?"

"Not well," she said. "I am afraid things do not look good at all."

"Did he do well with the move between the *Gypsy* and here, or do you think it may have worsened his condition?"

Isabel shook her head. "I do not know. I did not see him before he left your ship. I know only that he does not look well to me. He does not stop going in and out of"—she mumbled to herself in frustration—"I do not know how you say it . . . When you are conscious. *Conocimiento.*"

"Consciousness?" Adam offered.

"Yes, that is the word."

Of course he doesn't look well. Dr. Santos said not to move him.

Adam didn't say what he was thinking. Instead, he said, "Ma'am . . ." He caught himself. He didn't feel comfortable yet calling her a word that meant grandmother. "Was there anything else you wanted to tell me? I mean, was there a reason you had those men bring me here tonight? Or did you just want to let me know you believe me—that I'm . . . well . . . your grandson?"

"I thought you might wish to see him," she said. "And since he is so very poorly, I did not think that I should wait until the morning."

"Now?" he asked, unsure of whether he should get up and leave the room right then, or even if he did, how to get to the room where his father was resting.

Isabel stood and said, "Yes, now. Come with me."

ADAM FOLLOWED ISABEL OUT of the little chapel and up the stairs. The huge house was eerie at this hour. There were no servants up and working, no noise whatsoever.

Most of the place was in complete darkness, except for the areas illuminated by lanterns. One such area was the mahogany staircase. Once they reached the top of the stairs, Adam was not surprised when Isabel led him down a hallway to the left. Two rooms at the end of that corridor were illuminated, whereas the hallway that went to the right was pitch dark. Adam was soon able to see that one room looked like it was a guest bedroom that had been set up as a closet for the family physician's medical kit. The room just beyond that one on the left had an entryway that was catty-cornered, with only a thin strip of pale light coming from beneath the heavy wooden door.

Isabel opened the door and led Adam inside. There lay Santiago in an impressive mahogany bed that was covered by a gauzy canopy which went from the ceiling down to the floor. The double doors that led out to the balcony overlooking the sea were wide open, and a gentle breeze was blowing through. Adam couldn't help but be impressed, since he had never grown up with such a luxury. If he wanted to sleep with the windows open in warm weather, he had to contend with whatever biting insects came into the room.

There was a single sconce flickering with a tiny flame on the wall just inside the room. In spite of that being the only lamp that was lit, the room was still bright, because of the cool light of the waxing moon shining through the open window.

Although Santiago was silhouetted by the canopy, as Adam stepped forward, he could see that his father's forehead was beaded with sweat. Santiago was taking quick, shallow breaths as he slept. Adam didn't know what that meant medically, but it looked worrisome. He glanced at Isabel standing there beside him, as though she might be able to offer some explanation of her son's shallow breathing, but she just shook her head. Her eyes began to well with tears.

Instinctively, Adam put his arm around her. At five foot nine, he wasn't especially tall, but Isabel was still nearly eight inches shorter than him.

She leaned her head against his shoulder and wept, then dabbed her face with her handkerchief. "You be here with him now. There is no way to know if he will get better or how long he will be here with us."

Adam squeezed her shoulder, and then they looked at each other with a solemn understanding of the situation. Isabel excused herself from the room.

Adam sat down in a chair that was next to the bed. He imagined that Isabel was probably sitting there earlier when they first brought Santiago back to the estate. He was struck by the thought that when his father had left home the previous day to help Martin and Charlie find him, the man had no idea his rescue efforts were for his own son. And Santiago certainly would've never thought that it might be his last day to effortlessly move around and enjoy the beautiful grounds of the family's estate. Now he was striving against death itself as the effects of his injury attempted to extinguish whatever light of life remained within him.

Adam couldn't stop thinking about what Santiago had told him earlier—that he didn't want his son to watch him die. He pushed that thought out of his mind in an effort to mentally deny the fact that his father could be that close to death. Instead, he turned his thoughts to his mother. He wondered what she would think seeing her long-lost husband lying there in that condition. Would it break her heart? Or would she not care, since he left so many years ago and they had been apart for such a long time?

Nah, he thought. *My mama's a sensitive woman. She'd be in tears and worried sick to see him like this.*

Finally, Adam's thoughts drifted back to his father. *What*

would my life have been like if he never had to leave? I reckon it would've been so different.

He wondered what his mother would do if she were there. When he saw a basin of water on the dresser next to his bed and a stack of folded rags beside it, he knew. He grabbed one and dipped it in the water and used it to dab his father's forehead. His mother had always done that to him when he had a fever. Knowing it would likely have little effect, he leaned across the bed and dropped his head down onto his arm next to his father and sobbed quietly.

When a hand began to touch the top of his head, he was startled. He raised himself up and realized his father was awake.

"*Mijo* . . ." he said. "Am I dreaming? Or are you here."

Adam quickly dried his eyes and cleared his throat. "Yes, sir. I am here. I wanted to know how you were doing."

Santiago's eyes fluttered from open to closed. He looked like he was fighting hard to keep himself awake. "I am still alive but cannot say much more than that."

"Well, that's something," said Adam. "Thank God for it. You need to get better fast. We have a lot to talk about. There are so many things I want to ask you."

Santiago gave Adam a weak smile, then coughed. He looked like he was struggling to catch his breath.

Adam wondered if he should try to help him sit up. Lying there on his back for so long was probably causing congestion to pool in his lungs, and that might cause pneumonia. He tried to reach one hand under Santiago's right shoulder to help elevate him. His father didn't understand what he was trying to do at first and felt terrible pain in his left arm and shoulder from his injury.

"I'm trying to lift your head up a little," Adam explained.

"You'll be even worse off if your lungs start filling up with congestion."

Santiago gently closed his eyes in understanding. It appeared as though he found it too difficult to nod. He did try to lift himself a bit so that Adam could pull another pillow under his head and back. When he leaned over to help his father, he could feel heat radiating from his injured arm, but he didn't know if he should say anything to him or just wait and tell the doctor. He knew enough to recognize that meant an infection was setting in.

As soon as Santiago was more comfortably settled, he coughed strongly a few times, so much so that the sound of it worried Adam. He reached for another of the cloths on the bedside table and handed it to his father, who promptly used it to cover his mouth as he coughed up phlegm.

"I cannot understand why I am in this terrible state from just a gunshot wound to my arm," observed Santiago.

"I'm not sure," said Adam, "but if you have an infection starting, like the surgeon said, that could be making you feel bad all over."

"You have taken good care of me today, *mijo.*"

Adam forced a smile. "Of course. Well, I've tried." He took a moment to observe his father in his weakened state, then said, "It makes me so angry that this only happened because you were trying to rescue me. Not angry at you, of course, but at the situation. It makes me even angrier that Eduardo is the one to blame for keeping us apart all of these years."

"I understand." Santiago couldn't say much, but he looked like he was mustering every bit of strength he had to be able to talk to his son.

Adam was about to say something when Santiago spoke again. "You know, your mother . . ."

Adam wrinkled his brow, unsure of what his father would say. "Yes?"

"I want you to know I loved her with all my heart. I always . . ." He started coughing horribly again.

Adam grabbed the pitcher of water that was next to the basin on the dresser and poured some in a cup that was sitting next to it, and he gave it to his father.

After he had a sip, Santiago began to speak again. "I always hoped that maybe someday I would find a way to come back, but as the years went on, my uncle was still living, and I still did not trust him. And his *banda* seemed to always be growing more."

"I understand," said Adam. "But I have a question."

"What is it, *mijo?*"

"Do you think he'll keep coming after me now that he knows who I am?"

"Yes."

"Then what do you think I should do?" Adam's question was rhetorical. He knew his father barely had the strength to string a few words together, much less answer a question like that.

Nevertheless, Santiago pointed to a wardrobe on the far side of the room. "In there," he said.

Adam looked over and noticed the imposing piece of furniture. "You need something from there?"

Santiago nodded. "Yes, open it."

Adam crossed the room and pulled the heavy brass hoops that opened the doors. On the right there was a closet for hanging clothes, and on the left were several small drawers. He looked back at his father. "Now what?"

Santiago pointed to the left, indicating the drawers. "Third one" was all he said.

Adam opened the third drawer, but its contents were unremarkable—a large variety of men's stockings. He was surprised only because he'd never seen so many before outside of the general store back in Beaufort.

"Are your feet cold?" he asked his father.

Santiago tried to lift up his right arm to point downward. Adam took that to mean he should look in the drawer below. He opened that one, but it was only full of belt buckles and shoe buckles.

"No!" Santiago said. "Third drawer, beneath the socks."

Adam closed the fourth drawer and reopened the third one. He moved the socks aside but still didn't see anything.

"There's nothing here," he said. "I'm sorry, but I don't know what you want me to find here."

"Open it," said Santiago. "The drawer bottom."

Adam understood now. There had to be a secret compartment in the drawer. He felt around beneath the socks for any kind of latch or opening, but he wasn't able to feel anything but a solid piece of wood. He pulled a bunch of the socks out of the drawer and placed them in the right-hand side of the wardrobe, beneath the hanging clothes, then stood off to the side a bit so the moonlight could illuminate the inside of the drawer. Still no use.

"Use this," said Santiago, pointing to an unlit lantern on his bedside table.

Adam went over and grabbed the lantern and opened it, then spotted an ember bowl nearby on the dresser and used one of the tongs to pick up an ember and light the wick. He carried it over to the wardrobe and held the light over the drawer. He was finally able to see how it worked. There was a tiny pin on each side of the drawer that was holding the bottom in place. After he pulled each of them back, the bottom panel sprung up about an inch, just enough for Adam to be able to lift it out.

There were papers inside the drawer, including various envelopes.

"Take them," said Santiago.

Adam grabbed the stack of papers and brought them over to his father.

Santiago shook his head. "No, do not give them to me. You take them."

Adam wrinkled his brow. "What for?"

"My *testamento*—my will—is there, and letters from your mother." He smiled. "You will have to ask her if she still has the ones I sent to her."

Adam raised his eyebrows in surprise. He looked at the papers again, shocked at the idea of holding documents of such great importance and sentiment in his hands. Then something occurred to him. "It looks like most of the documents here are in Spanish. I can't read Spanish."

"Take them to Tomás. He can help you understand what is there."

Adam gave him a quizzical smile. "Thomas Drake? Even the letters from my mother?"

Santiago returned his grin. "You will be able to read those yourself. Those are in English."

"But you said your will is here. I don't think I should take this with me."

Santiago said, "You must. You are in mentioned in there, and I think it can solve your problem with Eduardo."

"I'm mentioned? But you didn't even know who I was until yesterday."

"I knew when I left Port Beaufort that my wife, your

mother, was carrying my child, and that is written in the document. You are not named in the document, but she is, and you are our son."

Adam looked down at the bundle of papers in his hand. He thought he knew which document was the will. He recognized the word *testamento*. If his father was sending that document with him, he must expect that he was not going to survive.

"Why would I take your will? You're going to make it through this. You're going to get better. You're strong, I know it."

Santiago shook his head. "Whether I do or not, just make sure my uncle knows about that document. Drake can help you find him."

Adam folded the will and stuck it in his pocket. The letters he bundled back up with a cord and placed on the dresser beside him. He sat back down in the chair next to the bed.

Santiago's eyelids were becoming heavy again.

"Don't go to sleep," said Adam. "Stay awake and we can talk. Or I'll talk—you can just listen."

His father was slow to respond, but he gave a nod and a weak smile. "Alright, *mijo*. I listen to you, but do not forget, I want you to leave here before I—"

"Stop talking like that! You keep talking like you're about to die or something. Don't do that!"

Adam could see that Santiago wanted to chuckle, but he could barely hold his eyes open. His chest went up almost as though he was trying to chuckle. "I just do not want you to see me . . ." His voice trailed off.

"Don't! Don't do that! What were you going to say?" Adam frantically tugged at his father's arm, trying to stir him to speak again. He was breathing, but it was almost as if he'd had a very limited supply of energy, and he'd just used it all up to have that brief conversation with his son.

Santiago's eyes weren't even open, but he was able to get out just a few more words: "I am so proud of you, my . . ." He drifted off to sleep again, and this time Adam could not stir him to wake.

He bowed his head on the mattress and prayed in a quiet voice, "God, why would you do this? Why would you bring me all the way here and then let all these terrible things happen? And now you're going to take my father? It's not fair! This is so wrong!" He continued in a diatribe against the Almighty, until he fell asleep with his head on his father's mattress.

After an hour or so, he looked up again, and his father was still sleeping, still drenched in sweat, and still breathing shallow. He thought about the things his father had said and how he didn't want Adam to watch him die, so he decided that first thing in the morning he had to find Drake.

He looked on the dresser and saw the bundle of letters. He grabbed them and stuffed them in his waistband under his shirt. Then he leaned over and smoothed back his father's hair off of his forehead and planted a kiss there. "God save you," he said, and then he turned and crept out of the room, down the hall, and out of the house.

Chapter Twenty

IT WAS STILL dark outside in spite of the brightness of the moon. Adam wanted to be sure and leave before Isabel or the rest of the household was awake.

Soon he made his way down the lane and out of the gate to the street. It was a long walk back to the *Gypsy*, but at least it had finally stopped raining. Adam knew as soon as he got there he'd do one of two things: either he'd start reading those letters that his mother had written to his father, or he'd fall fast asleep. It made little difference to him, as long as he knew he could get a decent night's rest in his berth until morning.

It seemed to take forever, but as he finally approached the wharf, he was struck by a great deal of commotion down near the warehouse where the *Gypsy* was moored. The nearer he got, the more concerned he became.

That chaos seemed to be coming from his own ship. His

slow and tired walk soon became a fast jog. There were men he recognized as shipmates coming up and down the ramp, and it appeared there were also some local men—or at least men he didn't recognize—also milling around by the bottom of the ramp of the *Gypsy*.

"What's happening here?" Adam asked the unfamiliar men.

They shrugged and said something to him in Spanish about *el capitán*.

As Adam made his way through the chaos up the ramp, he spotted Canady. "What's happened?" he asked.

"Some men came on board—I think from that group y'all met at that compound—and they nearly killed Ricky Jones."

Adam's eyes grew enormous. "What?" he said. "When did this—?"

"He and Smith are with the captain now. Go on up and see him."

"Good Lord!" Adam exclaimed. He was about to continue up the ramp when it dawned on him that Canady appeared to be leaving the ship. "Where are you going?"

"To get some air," said Canady, looking back towards the deck. "It's a madhouse up there."

At that, he scurried down the rest of the ramp and was soon out of sight. Meanwhile, Adam had boarded the vessel, and he was soon knocking on the door to the captain's quarters.

"What is it?" a voice inside demanded.

"It's Fletcher, Captain. I've come to check on Jones and Smith."

The door was quickly opened in his face. Martin was leaning against the back wall of the cabin.

"Come on in, come on in," said Captain Phillips, who

was standing over Jones, who was lying on the table in the captain's quarters, having a huge gash across his belly cleaned up.

"What happened here?" asked Adam.

"Do you even have to ask?" Martin chuckled. "It's that crazy family of yours."

Jones winced as the captain began stitching up the deepest part of the gash.

Adam waited until the captain finished and then asked Jones, "How did this happen? Were you out in town or something?"

Jones shook his head and put on a clean shirt, but he looked like he was too sore to talk.

Martin answered instead. "Uh-uh. We were all sleepin down below because of the rain. When me and Charlie and Jones got back from the tavern, Charlie passed out in Jones's berth—you know he ain't much of a drinker and he can't hold his liquor. Anyway, Jones, he saw you weren't in your berth, so he went to sleep there."

"Wait," said Adam. "Why did Jones get in my berth? Why didn't he just sleep in Charlie's?"

"Oh," said Martin, "because Charlie threw up in his right before he passed out in Jones's berth."

Adam nodded. "I see. Go on."

"I was sleepin in my own berth, of course," said Martin.

"So what happened then? You say this was my family?"

"Well, they weren't your family members—at least not that I know of—but this happened because of all that crazy mess with your daddy and your uncle."

"What in the world, Jones?!" said Adam. "Did they just pounce on you or something? Did they think you were me?"

"I reckon they assumed I was, mate," said Jones, "because your sea chest was right there, and it said 'A. Fletcher.'"

Adam tipped his head to the side, feeling stupid for asking the question. That was how the Velasquez family servants had found him earlier that same night.

"Yeah," said Martin, "and anyway it was dark, and you and Jones look right similar when you get down to it."

"Anyhow," said Jones, "I was just sleepin, you know? Real good, actually—and next thing I know, one of them scoundrels had his hand over my mouth and the other one was about to stab me with a dagger. I moved quick, though, and got out from under him just in time. Ended up with this gash instead."

"Good Lord! Then what happened? I guess both of you saw 'em?"

Jones nodded. "Unfortunately."

Martin said, "I did. They were a couple of those men from Eduardo's compound. I remember seein them there. One of 'em was that Hector fella."

"Hector?" Adam exclaimed. "Eduardo must've sent 'em! He should've been able to tell that Jones wasn't me, though!"

"Well, like I told you," said Martin, "you and Jones are both real similar in height and hair color and whatnot, so in the dark down here, and with that sea chest sayin 'A. Fletcher,' I'm sure he just thought it was you."

Adam turned his head away in frustration. "That man is relentless!" He thought for a moment, then said, "What happened to the men who attacked you?"

Martin's eyes grew big. "What do you reckon happened? They sure won't be pullin any more stunts like that. As soon as all the fellas down below realized what was happenin, we all came down on those two boys like dogs on a fox."

"Were they arrested?"

Martin looked at Adam as though he had lost his mind. "Arrested? I reckon they're probably gettin the grand tour of Hell right about now."

"They're dead?"

Martin nodded. "Of course they're dead. What do you think? You've got two men breakin onto this ship in the middle of the night, and here they were, tryin to kill one of the crew. Those boys weren't about to walk out of here alive. And let's face it: it ain't like we could've just turned them over to the sheriff."

"Where are they now?" asked Adam.

"Don't ask," said Jones. "You really don't wanna know, mate."

Adam had no idea what that meant, and he wasn't going to press any further. He understood their situation and knew they did whatever was necessary to protect everybody on board.

"I wonder if Eduardo knows about it yet . . . I wonder if it will make him back off." Adam was stunned that all this had happened in just the few hours he was away. He considered what might have been the case if he had been in the berth instead of Jones when those men came. He'd like to think he'd have been able to thwart their attack, like Jones did, but as tired as Adam was, he didn't know that his responses would have been as quick.

Martin leveled his gaze at him and said, "Men like that are dispensable to men like Eduardo. Even though those two are dead, he's got a whole army ready to fall right in behind him as soon as he says the word. This ain't gonna stop, boy, and you know it."

"I know." Adam took a deep breath, sighed, and then kicked the ground. "Do you know my father just gave me his will tonight? He wanted me to make sure I had it. Said it will put an end to all of this mess with Eduardo."

"He gave you his will?" Martin wrinkled his brow. "Is he about to die or somethin? What's it say?"

Adam shrugged. "How should I know? It's in Spanish, for goodness' sake! But he said Drake could tell me and help me find Eduardo so I can get it to him."

"What?" Martin was aghast. "He wants to send you back into the belly of the beast?"

"He didn't mean for me to have to go back to the compound. I think he meant for me to take this to Eduardo somewhere here in town. So that's exactly what I'm going to do."

ADAM AND MARTIN STOOD in Drake's parlor as he sat in his favorite chair and read out loud from his friend's will.

"I, Santiago Rogelio Velasquez de Leon . . . blah, blah, blah . . . Let's see here . . ." Drake scanned through the document quickly while Adam and Martin hovered over his shoulder.

"Well, what does it say?" asked Adam. "I know it doesn't say 'blah, blah, blah.'"

Drake waved his hand and motioned at the first two paragraphs of the document and said, "The beginning is just the long formal introduction where he says who he is and that he commits his body back to the earth and prays that his soul will go to God, who created him, and so forth . . . Ah . . . let's see . . ."

He continued to scan down the page until he came to something that caused him to wrinkle his brow in surprise. "Oh, good heavens," Drake mumbled under his breath as he continued reading.

Adam and Martin both looked at each other.

Adam said to Drake, "What? What is it?"

"I think . . ." Drake ran his finger along the three lines of text again and again, as if he wanted to make sure he was understanding it correctly. "I think it says, 'To my wife, Mary Fletcher of the Town of Beaufort, in the County of Carteret, in the Province of North Carolina, I give all of the contents of the small chest that I keep locked in the bureau on my sloop, *La Dama del Caribe*, which consists of several mementos that would be of personal value to her. To the child that was born to me by my wife, the aforementioned Mary Fletcher, provided the child is living at the execution of this document, I give my sloop, *La Dama del Caribe*. If that child is not still living at the execution of this document, the sloop should be offered to Mary Fletcher, or if she prefers, it should be sold, and she should be given the proceeds of that sale.'"

Adam gasped, but he didn't know what to say.

"Wait, there's more here," said Drake. "And this is where it gets really interesting!"

Adam raised his eyebrows and exchanged a look of surprise with Martin. "Well, go ahead. Keep reading."

Drake continued: "Listen to this: 'It has come to my attention that my uncle, Eduardo Velasquez de Castillo, has called into question my legitimacy and has said that I am not the son of his brother, Juan Diego Velasquez de Castillo. As much as it grieves me to say so, I have determined by investigations of my own that my uncle's charge is likely to be correct. While I am unable to disclose my exact sources, I can say that I learned this information through interviews with a few individuals whose identities I swore to keep secret. I also have reason to believe that Juan Diego Velasquez de Castillo, the man I have always known as my father, also knew the truth about my paternity . . .'" Drake continued reading and said, "He just goes on here to explain that because of the aforementioned information, he relinquishes his rights to any portion of the Velasquez estate to which he is entitled by the will of his father, and that he would hand it over directly for the benefit of the sons of his Uncle Eduardo, except that it is presently in the possession of his mother, Isabel, to be held during her widowhood for the benefit of Santiago."

The three men looked at each other, stunned.

"Did that really just say he gives up the entire Velasquez estate?" Martin asked.

"That must be what he meant about this would fix everything," Adam mused. "But my father isn't dead yet, and neither is my grandmother."

Drake shook his head. "You're right. I'm not so certain this is going to soothe the beast. Eduardo of all people would know that as long as Santiago lives, he can potentially change the will. Also, Santiago has not yet received the full balance of the estate, because Isabel is still living. He cannot give away something that does not yet belong to him."

"Maybe he just thought that if Eduardo knew his intentions—and this was written before I ever even arrived in Havana—he would back off," Adam suggested.

"But then why wouldn't he have just shown it to ol' Eddie a long time ago and then gone back to Beaufort to be with you and your mama?" asked Martin.

"Think. Just think about it," Adam said. "He didn't want to let his uncle know that me and my mother survived that fire if he didn't have to, so I reckon he just drew up the will and held on to it in case he did die before his mother. I guess he wanted to make sure he could leave something for me and my mother—and that whole business about giving me *La Dama del Caribe*, I don't even know what to make of that, because I sure don't know how to captain my own ship. Then of course he wanted to give the Velasquez inheritance to his uncle's children—*not* his uncle. That was all Eduardo ever cared about, anyway."

"He's a clever chap, Santiago," said Drake. "Let me look to see when this thing is dated . . ." He studied the document again and then said, "June 1748."

"That was just a few months after I was born," said Adam. "I can't believe he's had this drawn up that whole time."

"Well, just be happy he has," said Martin.

ADAM, MARTIN, AND DRAKE stood in front of the steps to the enormous double doors of the residence of the high sheriff, which was where Eduardo lived with his family. They were careful and brought a few of their shipmates from the *Gypsy* in case the tense meeting came to violence.

"Alright, fellas," Adam said to Martin and Drake. "This is it."

He went up the steps and pounded the heavy knocker against the door three times before a man answered it.

"*Buenos dias,*" said the man.

"I need to see Eduardo."

The man looked at Adam with a quizzical expression and said, "*Un momento, por favor.*" Then he disappeared behind the door and into the house.

When the door opened again, Eduardo was standing there.

"What do you want?" he asked Adam, his tone abrupt.

Adam held up the document in his hand. "I think I have something you might want to see."

Eduardo tried to snatch the document out of his hand, but Adam quickly pulled it down and stuck it in his pocket.

"I want you to look over there," said Adam, pointing to Martin and Drake, "and over there." He pointed to the group of men who were gathered behind him on the cobblestone street.

Martin and Drake both waved at Eduardo. The others weren't as friendly and instead just scowled at him.

"What is the meaning of all of this?" said Eduardo. "Do you think you can intimidate me in my own home?"

"That isn't the point of any of this," said Adam. "This is just to show you some of the men who are here today, who are going to make sure that I leave here better off than my friend Jones over there fared after your men tried to stab him last night, and better off than my father is back at his house."

"What do you want?" Eduardo demanded. "I do not have time for your childish games."

"How about let's go on inside and talk? I don't reckon we need to air all of this business out here on the streets."

Eduardo narrowed his eyes at Adam and then opened his door and motioned for him to come inside. Adam turned back and waved for Drake and Martin to come as well.

Eduardo tried to stop them from entering by closing the door, but Adam put his foot in the way and forced it back open. "Uh-uh," he said. "They're coming too."

Martin and Drake pushed their way in, and there the four of them were—Adam, Eduardo, Martin, and Drake—all standing in the foyer of Eduardo's huge house.

"Aren't you going to invite us in to sit, Uncle?" said Adam.

Eduardo was fuming but obviously in no position to protest. He led the three men into his office and motioned for them to sit. Adam and Drake sat in the two chairs in front of the desk.

Martin pulled a third chair over from against the wall and sat with them. Eduardo sat in his own chair behind the desk.

"Fine," said Eduardo. "We are all here. We are all sitting. Now what do you want?"

Adam took the folded-up piece of paper out of his pocket and dropped it on Eduardo's desk. "Here ya go."

"*¿Que es esto?*" he asked.

"You'll see," said Drake.

Eduardo unfolded the paper and smoothed it out on his desk and began reading. As soon as he realized it was a will, in a mocking tone he asked, "Is my poor nephew dead already?"

"Not yet." Adam's eyes twitched. He involuntarily made fists, but he squeezed his own thumbs to keep his hands busy rather than diving across the desk and wringing the man's neck, which was what he really wanted to do. "Now you just keep reading."

As Eduardo continued to read, a small smile crept across his face. He said, "This is very nice, but it matters little, since Santiago is still alive."

Adam forcefully waved at the paper. "Look at the date on the document. This was written eighteen years ago. It looks to me like he decided a long time ago that you were too crazy to reason with, so he was already prepared to give you what you want. Your heirs will have the Velasquez estate. Do you honestly think he's going to rewrite this in the condition he's in?"

Eduardo looked up and locked eyes with Adam. "I am not sure that I want to take a chance on that."

"What's that supposed to mean?" said Adam.

"I do believe that was a threat, lad," said Drake.

Eduardo said nothing but only closed and opened his

eyes slowly and sighed the way someone might do if they were especially bored.

"You aren't going to lay a finger on him," said Adam. He snatched the document up from the desk and folded it back up and put it in his pocket. "I'm going to make sure of that."

"And tell me, *chico*, what will you do? You will not always be here in Havana, will you?"

"You best think that through, Ed," said Drake. "As it stands right now, your sons will inherit the Velasquez estate when Santiago dies, whether it's days from now or decades. Right now, with this document you're still getting what you want. You start throwing out a bunch of threats—just you remember we can destroy that document as easily as it was for us to bring it to you. Without a will, everything that Santiago stands to inherit will pass directly to Adam and his mother."

Eduardo intentionally ignored Drake. Instead, he kept his eyes fixed on Adam. "Tell me, *chico*, how are you still alive? I thought for sure you would no longer be a problem for me."

"I never have been a problem for you, Eduardo. Only in your own imagination have I ever been a problem for you. When I came to Havana, the only thing I wanted to do was learn something about my father, but little did I know I was walking right into a trap. You're an absolute lunatic! You had me kidnapped. Your men nearly killed me. They ended up shooting my father, and now he's fighting for his life. Then you almost killed a friend because those two idiots who work for you didn't bother to double-check who they were going to stab. And now *those* men are dead because you sent them to do your dirty work."

Eduardo pressed his palms into his desk as he leaned across it to face Adam. "Listen to me, *chico*. Listen very well. I will do whatever it takes to make sure you do not rob my sons of what is rightfully theirs."

"Are you even listening to me? *I never wanted anything here.* I never even knew there was anything to want! The way I see it, you've only been able to succeed at three things these last few days: One, you've made yourself look like a complete ass. Two, you've sent two of your own men to their death. And three, you and your men may have killed the son of your own brother."

Eduardo stood from his desk and slammed his hands down on the top of it. "That is just it! Do you not understand! Your father is a bastard! My brother was *not* his father. My brother never even slept with his wife, Isabel. Your father is the child of Isabel and the English lover of her youth. I know it because I was there in the house when her visitor came and took her to bed, the whore!"

Something in Adam snapped. He had heard just about enough of that word thrown around. He stood from his chair so forcefully it fell backwards.

"I'm done here," said Adam. "You've seen the will. The estate will be yours. Now just leave us all alone and stay out of our lives. You are *nothing* to me."

Eduardo did not respond.

Adam looked at Martin and Drake. "You ready?"

He left the office and the residence, and his friends were right behind him. As soon as he got out into the street, the others were waiting there and accompanied Adam and Martin back to Plaza Vieja for something to eat before deciding on their next move.

Chapter Twenty-One

AFTER THEY LEFT Eduardo's, Drake went back home, and Martin went out to have a drink with a couple of other shipmates from the *Gypsy*.

Adam wasn't up for socializing, though. He decided to head on back to the ship so he could try to make sense of everything that had happened. He wanted to feel confident that Eduardo would no longer be a problem, but the truth was he wasn't sure. On one hand, the man could have been just blustering when he said he might not want to wait for Santiago to die. On the other hand, he had already proven himself to be completely irrational and ready to do just about anything to make sure he secured the family's estate for his sons. The only thing that gave Adam any consolation was knowing that Eduardo had heretofore been restrained by at least some small thread of conscience when it came to actually killing any of his Velasquez family members.

There was one thing that he knew now with certainty, though: Santiago truly had made every decision of the last eighteen years in a calculated effort to protect his wife and child. He was willing to do whatever it took to keep Eduardo out of their lives. Adam hated that he had grown up without a father, but he understood now, as unfair as it seemed, why things had to be the way they were.

As soon as he ascended the ramp up on to the *Gypsy*, he saw Captain Phillips on the quarterdeck with Charlie, sea charts spread out, plotting the navigation course for the return trip.

Adam knew right away what that meant. It was time for them to go back home.

"Good afternoon, Captain."

"Good day to you, Mr. Fletcher."

Adam walked over to where the two men stood and briefly studied the charts, although he still wasn't very clear on how to read them. "I reckon this means we'll be leaving soon?"

"Yes, we will," said the captain. He turned to speak more directly with Adam. "Now listen, I don't make it a habit of explainin decisions to crew members, but given the circumstances—and this bein your first time on a voyage like this—I feel I might ought to explain."

Adam humbly narrowed his eyes and shook his head. "No, sir. I understand. There's no need to explain."

But Captain Phillips seemed determined to explain anyway. "You realize we're already real behind. The repairs are done now, and I hate to tell you this, but I think there's some real rough weather that's headed this way. We need to move on out of here and stay ahead of what's comin, or we may not make it back at all."

Adam nodded. The whole situation felt awkward. To know that he had at least some part in causing a whole ship and her crew to be delayed in port for a few days embarrassed him. Sure, there were repairs that needed to be made, but those were done a day ago—and they might have been done even earlier if Martin and the others hadn't gotten sidetracked with that whole ransom and kidnapping business.

"We'll be leaving at daybreak, Mr. Fletcher."

Adam nodded once more and excused himself to go below deck to rest in his berth and ponder the captain's news.

It was not really unexpected, but it left Adam feeling anxious nevertheless. The truth was, part of him felt like he should stay, given his father's condition, but every time he thought about the *Gypsy* returning to Beaufort without him on it and what that would do to his mother, especially considering the history with his father, he knew he had no choice but to resign himself to the captain's decision. He consoled himself by remembering there was nothing he could do about Eduardo, considering he *was* the law. Who could he go to with his concerns about threats to his father's safety? He reminded himself there was nothing that could be done about the estate situation or his father's seemingly deteriorating state of health. Maybe it was all for the best, he thought. *At least this takes the decision out of my hands.*

Since it was still relatively early in the day, Adam knew he should probably head on back to his father's estate so he could let them know he would be leaving. He prayed his father wouldn't be any worse.

When he told Captain Phillips that he planned to go see his family before he left, the captain told him to wait for Martin or somebody else to go with him. Fortunately, Martin and the others got back within the hour. Apparently, they had only had one round of drinks at El Trobador before returning to the vessel. If they had known they'd set sail the next morning, they'd have surely stayed a while longer.

As soon as Adam heard their voices on the main deck, he went up to talk to Martin.

"I need to go back to the estate for a little while. Cap'n says he doesn't want me to go without somebody, so will you go?"

Martin scratched at his sandy curls as he thought about his answer. "Did he say *I* had to go with you? 'Cause I'm gonna tell you right now I'm worn slam out. And to tell you the truth, I really just don't feel like it. I don't think I can take any more of your Velasquez family madness *today*."

"Very funny," Adam said. "Just come with me, alright? What if something happens to me and here we are about to leave? Mr. Rogers will have your tail."

Martin gave a sideways glance and sighed. "Fine."

The two descended the ramp off the vessel and headed back into the city. Adam noticed Martin was in a foul mood. That was unusual enough as it was, because he usually had a relaxed and joking personality, but it was even more unusual because he had been drinking, and that was typically a surefire way to lift his spirits.

"What's wrong with you, anyway?" Adam asked. "You act like something's got you all riled up."

Martin exhaled sharply but didn't say anything.

"You don't look like you been in a fight. The only time I ever see you acting like this is either if you've been fighting or if it's about a girl."

Martin narrowed his eyes at Adam in an irritated look.

Adam gave him a tense, knowing smile. "Ahh . . . It is about a girl. What did you do?"

"What the hell's wrong with you?" Martin spat. "First you figure it's about a girl. Next you're figurin it's something I did. You're really some friend, you know that?" he said as he sped up and walked ahead.

Adam picked up his pace to catch up with him. "So it wasn't about a girl?"

"I didn't say that," said Martin. "Stop trying to guess at things you don't know anything about!"

"Oh." Adam decided not to push the matter any further. Whatever it was, it had Martin angrier than he'd ever seen him.

They continued walking for a few minutes in complete silence. As they walked down the street where the estate was located, Martin started volunteering information. "Yes, it was a girl. In fact, it was *the* girl—the one from the other night."

"What happened?"

"Turns out that little *strumpet* was working for Eduardo."

Adam's eyes widened. "What? How did you find this out?"

"Ahh." Martin waved his hand dismissively. "Jones admitted it to me when we were all drinking. He said he had heard Eduardo tell her in Spanish to show you a good time and keep you at her place as long as she could."

"When and how would Jones have heard all of that?"

"Don't you remember? When we all sat down and then Eduardo came in, he said something to her in Spanish. I didn't understand what it was, but I reckon he was telling her to do this thing and he'd pay her the next day. That's why she didn't make me pay her—and here I thought she just liked me."

"And you're angry about this?" Adam asked. "You're actually *angry* about this?"

"Damn right I'm angry," said Martin.

Adam could guess why, but he decided to ask him anyway—for fun. "Why would you be angry?"

Martin looked at Adam as though he would have to be an idiot for asking such a question. After a moment Adam elbowed him in the side so that he'd realize he was just joking around, trying to lighten up the situation.

The gates of the estate were coming into view.

Adam said, "So I reckon when Eduardo overheard me telling you to meet me the next morning, he must've decided then to pay that prostitute to keep you busy so it would either keep me from going off in search of Alonso Cordova, or else it would've meant I'd likely be waiting for you there alone, and it would make me an easy mark for Hector."

"And I fell for it all the way," said an exasperated Martin.

"Well, that part is behind us now. Maybe it'll teach you something about trifling with prostitutes."

WHEN THEY ARRIVED AT the gate to the Velasquez estate, they were immediately permitted entrance by Felipe and shown right inside. The servant who answered the door to the main house went in to let Señora Isabel know that Adam had arrived, but she did not come out to greet him. Instead, the servant took Adam straight to his father's room upstairs. Martin was instructed to wait in the foyer.

In the harsh light of day that was streaming through the window, Adam could see Santiago was wasting away. Without the ability to eat or drink, he looked haggard, as though his body were feasting upon itself. *Maybe that's why he didn't want me to see him like this*, Adam thought. Even the night before, the light of the moon softened the harshness of Santiago's weakened appearance. He was but a shadow now of the strong and handsome young captain who had given Adam that sack of candy and fireworks at Laney Martin's dock.

Adam sat in the chair next to the bed, then bowed his head and prayed over his father. He tried to speak to him, but Santiago did not respond. After a few more minutes Adam wondered if his father's spirit hadn't already gone. It was as though the body lying there in the bed was little more than a shell.

Finally, he stood from his chair and leaned over and brushed the long, wavy hair away from his father's forehead and planted a kiss there one last time. "I'm leaving soon. I just want to tell you that I love you," he whispered. "And I'll always remember you."

He observed his father for another moment or two, just to see if there might be any sort of response, but there was none. He knew it was time to leave.

Just as he opened the door, a figure was blocking the doorway. It took him a couple of seconds to register that it was Eduardo.

Adam froze. He made the almost instantaneous decision that he would not move from the doorway to let Eduardo through.

"What are you doing here?" he demanded. "No, even more to the point—who let you in?"

"Do you think the servants here do not do exactly as I say? They know enough to fear me. Now move yourself, *chico!*"

He tried to push past the muscular young man. When

Adam stood his ground and refused to move, Eduardo quickly pulled out a pistol from his belt and held it in Adam's face.

"I said *move*, or I will blow off your head."

Adam knew better than to argue with a gun. Before he stepped aside, though, he said to Eduardo, "If you came here to kill your nephew, I think you'll find you're probably already too late."

He took a couple of steps back to let Eduardo come in, and watched as he rushed over to the side of his father's bed, pistol still in hand.

Eduardo looked as if he was examining Santiago. He watched his body to see if there was any movement. He lowered his head over Santiago's chest to listen for a heartbeat and held his fingers under Santiago's nose, presumably so he could try and determine whether he was breathing. Finally, he whipped his head around and glared at Adam.

"I told you. You're too late," Adam said. "You won't get the privilege of taking his life. Now your sons will get their precious estate, and maybe you can leave us all alone."

"No." Eduardo crossed the room to stand about a foot away from Adam. "No, I do not think you understand. Isabel still lives." He flipped out his hand with the pistol in it and turned it again towards Adam, this time loosely pointed at his chest. "And most unfortunately, *you* still live."

"So what? Are you going to kill both of us?" Adam asked.

Eduardo shook his head. "No, it is not necessary. If you are dead, she has no heir. You must understand, my *nephew* never received Isabel's part of the Velasquez properties, and so his will is worthless. He cannot give to me something that he does not possess. So as it stands, you would naturally inherit everything when Isabel dies."

"And I have already told you there is *nothing* here that I want. *Nothing.* Why can't you seem to get that through your thick, stupid skull?"

Adam realized after the words left his mouth that he probably shouldn't be throwing insults at an armed man intent on seeing him dead, and yet he couldn't help himself. And he didn't regret saying what he had. In fact, there was more he wanted to say, but Eduardo's response came too quickly.

"You are the stupid one." He stepped forward, pistol in hand, leaving Adam no choice but to back up. "You are nothing but a worthless English apprentice from a worthless little American colony—the son of a worthless barmaid. You are not even intelligent enough to understand what it would have meant to you to be a part of this family."

Adam realized Eduardo was backing him right up to the side of his father's bed. He thought about how useless his little pocketknife was in the current circumstances and tried to calculate an exit from the situation, since he knew Eduardo's goal was to end his life. He also thought about Isabel. What would Eduardo do to her?

"Let me ask you a question," Adam said. "Why did you bring a pistol? Isn't that a little more than necessary, considering the circumstances? Why not just use a knife? Or even just strangle him? Afraid of getting your hands too dirty? Or maybe you don't know that you could go through with it or finish the job."

Eduardo continued to wave the pistol around in Adam's face. "You talk like you are such a brave boy. If you even knew what a fortune you were losing, you would not be standing here so calm as you are. You would be devastated to lose such a treasure. You are not even smart enough to be upset about the fact that I am going to take your life."

Adam shook his head. "Now see there. You've got it all wrong."

Eduardo flashed a smug smile at Adam, as though he expected the boy to start begging for his life or something.

He was wrong. Adam smiled back and said, "You're not going to take my life. You don't have that power."

Eduardo's face twitched as Adam continued: "See, what you're after—it's fool's gold. It's like that dew on the grass in the morning. Oh, it sparkles a little while to be sure, but as soon as the sun starts shining on it, it all dries right up. You place money and property above everything—above family, even above God Almighty. You know that puts you in a precarious spot . . . and it's sad, really." Adam figured there was no reason to stop now. He might as well say what he was thinking until the man pulled the trigger. "Didn't anybody ever teach you that the love of money is the root of all evil? If you fire that pistol and kill me, you'll only accomplish two things: helping me get to Heaven quicker, and securing your own place in Hell."

Just then Eduardo cocked the pistol and was about to fire, but before he could, Adam grabbed his wrist and pushed his hand back. They wrestled for a few seconds, and then Eduardo fired the pistol. Much to Adam's surprise, the man collapsed on top of him.

At first, Adam couldn't tell if the pistol had misfired and injured Eduardo, or if the lead ball had somehow gone past him into the mattress. When he looked over Eduardo's slumped body, he saw there was a knife in his back, and Isabel was standing right behind him.

Adam carefully pushed Eduardo off of him, and he wrapped his arms around Isabel. She began to sob against his shoulder.

"Shh . . ." Adam hugged her with one arm and stroked the back of her head with the other. "Don't worry. Everything will be fine. Shh . . ."

At first, she was muttering something in Spanish frantically and through tears, and then she appeared to remember that Adam couldn't understand Spanish.

"He was about to kill you," she said. She looked to Adam as if she was trying very hard to be strong and regain her composure. "I could not let him kill my grandson. And look!" She motioned at Santiago in the bed. "Do you see? Is my son already dead?"

Adam looked back at his father and then let go of Isabel so he could lean down and check on him again.

"Not quite," he told her. "I know he seems very close—close enough that Eduardo was fooled—but he has been doing this ever since I got here. His breathing is very shallow; then it seems to stop; then it's very shallow again."

"I need to send for the priest, then," said Isabel.

She wept as she left the room. Adam followed close behind her, and as they neared the stairs, Martin and the shorter of the two Spanish servants who had gone to the *Gypsy* to get Adam the night before were running up to meet them.

"What the hell happened?" asked Martin. "We heard a shot." He looked at Adam and Isabel, then tried to look past them down the hall.

"It was Eduardo. He showed up out of nowhere," said Adam. "He was about to kill me, but my *abuela* here stopped him before he could. She saved my life."

Isabel paid no attention to Adam or Martin but instead told her servant something in Spanish, to which he immediately responded, "*Claro, señora. Venga conmigo.*" He held out his arm for her to steady herself and escorted her down the stairs.

Adam and Martin watched as she walked away.

"What was that about?" said Martin.

"I think she's going to get the priest."

"For Eduardo?"

Adam shook his head. "Uh-uh. It's my father. He's . . ." His voice trailed off as he tried to bring himself to say what was happening.

They were both still standing at the top of the stairs. Martin looked back down the hall and said, "Well, should we go back in there?"

"No." Adam started to walk down to the first floor and motioned for Martin to follow. "In fact, I need to get out of here. I promised him."

"You promised him what?"

"I promised him I wouldn't stick around to watch him die."

"What about Eduardo? Is he . . . still alive?"

"I don't think so," said Adam as he got to the bottom of the stairs and crossed the foyer to see if he could tell which way his grandmother had gone.

A black servant saw him craning his head to look in different rooms and said, "*La señora se fue por allí.*" He motioned down the hallway that led to the family chapel.

Adam motioned for Martin to wait for him in the foyer again. Martin rolled his eyes, clearly frustrated with all of this waiting around.

When he came to the entryway to the family chapel, Adam looked in and saw Isabel sitting in the same place she had been sitting in the previous night.

"*Abuela,*" he said. "May I come in?"

Isabel turned around, but she could not look at her grandson. She only held out her hand and motioned for him to come sit beside her again on the pew. She continued to hold her hand out as he came nearer, so he could tell she wanted him to hold her hand, which he did.

"I don't know how I can ever thank you for what you did back there," he said. "You were so . . . brave. The way you came in and just stopped him"—Adam snapped his fingers—"like that!"

"Timoteo has gone for the priest—to bring him here so he can give my son the last rites. I will have to confess it to him when he comes," she said. "Murder is a mortal sin. I do not know if he can even forgive me of such a thing."

"Murder?" Adam exclaimed. "You were defending my life! I'm your grandson. I don't know anything about your priest or what he can or can't do, but I know for a fact God can forgive you—not that you need forgiving! It was self-defense!"

"You do not understand," she said. "I am not sorry that I killed him. And I am glad he is dead. He was an evil man. If I had known about all of this—about you—for all of these many years, maybe I would have even killed him in a storm of anger long ago."

"Well, I'm happy you didn't," said Adam. "That *would* have been a whole different situation. And anyway, the fact that you're relieved that he's dead—this man who's been tormenting your family and keeping it apart for eighteen years—I don't remember anything in the Bible that says you're supposed to feel sad about the death of someone like that. Just let God deal with Eduardo."

Isabel continued to hold on to her grandson with her left hand and dabbed at her eyes with her handkerchief with her right.

"Listen to me again," Adam insisted. "You saved my life up there. If you hadn't come in when you did and stopped him, I'd be dead now, and he might would've come after you next!"

Isabel seemed to consider what he said for a moment, and then she gave him a slight nod in agreement.

"I am grateful to you," he said.

After another moment or two of silence between them, Adam immediately thought about Eduardo's body up in his father's room. When the priest arrived, what would he think about seeing a man with a knife in his back on the floor there?

"¿Abuela?" he asked. "Should we, well . . . should we remove Eduardo's body from the room?"

Isabel waved her hand with the handkerchief in it dismissively and said, "Do not worry. My servants are taking him out of the room now. They are putting him in another room until we inform his family."

After another brief period of silence, Adam asked, "How did you know? I mean, you came at exactly the right time."

Isabel looked straight ahead at the altar as she answered him: "When Eduardo made the servants let him in, naturally they came right to tell me about it. I suspected there might be trouble, so I went up there to see. The door was open, and I saw him backing you across the room. As soon as I realized what was happening, I did not even think about it. I just came up behind him and I brought the blade down into his back."

"How did you know to bring the knife? I mean, why didn't you ask one of your servants to come with you."

"I always have my knife," she said, patting the waistline of her dress. "I have a little pocket in here and a little thing to cover it in." She looked at Adam as though she was trying to teach him something. "My father always instructed me to carry it to keep myself safe. I have had it since I was a girl. I never had to use it for anything like that, though." She thought for a moment and stuck her hand into the pocket, which was really just a slit in her dress that allowed her to access the "pockets" that she wore on a belt around her waist. "I must remember to get my knife back."

She made that last comment with such seriousness and in such an unexpected way that Adam had to try hard not to chuckle. He also was amused at how she characterized it as a little pocket and a little thing to put the knife in, because the knife surely did not look little to him.

"Do you want me to go tell Eduardo's family?" he asked.

Isabel shook her head. "No. That would not be a good idea. They are not crazy people like Eduardo was, but they will still be very upset, and they do not know you at all. It is best that we keep it that way, I think."

Adam nodded. "I understand."

"In fact," she said, "I think you should go now." She stood from the pew and encouraged Adam to do the same.

Adam stood up and said, "Are you sure? I can stay here with you right now."

"No," she said, "I want you to go. When are you leaving?"

"Cap'n says we're leaving first thing in the morning."

"Well, please ask him to let you come here very shortly first. I will give you some money to take to him now to make it worth his trouble. It should not take us very long, but there is something we need to discuss."

"I'll see what I can do," said Adam.

Isabel walked with him back into the foyer, but not before stepping briefly into a little closet along the hallway and coming out with a small bag filled with coins. "I think your captain will not mind waiting an hour or two if you give him this."

Adam raised his eyebrows and gave a half smile, then said, "I don't know. We'll see."

He reached down and gave her a hug. After that, he and Martin left to return to the *Gypsy* once more.

Chapter Twenty-Two

"WHAT TOOK Y'ALL so long?" The captain wasted no time expressing his frustration with Adam and Martin when they came back on the vessel. "I thought you was only goin to say your farewells to your family."

"I'm sorry, Cap'n," said Adam. "But we—"

Martin quickly interrupted him and told the captain, "His father looked awful, and his grandmother was havin a terrible time lettin him go."

The captain looked at Adam and grinned. "Is that so? I reckon you must've made quite an impression on the old woman, 'specially considering she didn't even know she had a grandson."

Adam looked at Martin, grateful his friend didn't mention *all* of what happened. Then he directed his attention back at the captain. "Yeah, well, she was pretty emotional. She said I look just like my father when he was my age . . . and now with him so bad off and all . . . Well, you understand."

"Yeah, I reckon I understand. It's late, though. Y'all go on and get your mess together and go to sleep. We're leavin shortly after sunup."

Adam looked down, then out across the harbor before he said, "About that . . ."

Captain Phillips looked at Martin first, then Adam, as if he was wondering what kind of news he was about to be hit with. "You ain't about to tell me that you're stayin here, are you, Fletcher? 'Cause I'm afraid I just cannot let you do that. Emmanuel will kill me first, then your mama'll come after me."

Adam chuckled and shook his head. "No, Cap'n. It's nothin like that. My grandmother just wants me to come back by the house early in the morning before we leave. She said it won't delay us more than an hour or two. Said she needed to talk to me about something."

"I hate to tell you this, son, but I just can't let you do that. Every time you leave this ship, you end up gettin back late. We can't afford that kind of delay in the morning—I told you already."

"But she told me to give you this." Adam pulled the pouch out of his pocket and held it out for the captain. "She said this would compensate you for your trouble."

Captain Phillips wrinkled his brow and then took the pouch. He pulled open the string and looked inside and appeared to visually count at least part of the contents. He closed the bag back tight, and his eyes grew huge. He looked off in the distance, as if he couldn't believe what he'd just seen, then grinned and said, "You're foolin with me, I can tell. Ain't no way that woman sent this much gold just to ask me to stay in port an extra hour or two."

Adam nodded enthusiastically. "No, she did! She said it was real important that I go by in the morning—that it wouldn't take long. Maybe it has to do with legal things or something, because of my father's condition and all. She was too upset to talk about it while we were there." He looked at his friend to back him up. "Isn't that right, Martin?"

Martin nodded. "Indeed. He's tellin the truth, Cap'n. I'll go back over there with him in the mornin, and I assure you I'll have him back here no later than nine o'clock."

Adam could see the captain considering the offer before he finally agreed.

"Alright. I'll let you go, but I'm holding this to pay Emmanuel, in case we end up losing his other customers for being late. Lord willing, we can still outrun that weather."

Adam and Martin nodded in agreement.

"Lord willing," said Adam.

The captain took the pouch and put it in his pocket.

SHORTLY BEFORE SUNSET, THE captain had sent out Jones and Willis with some money to go round up some meat, vegetables, and bread, along with a bunch of mangoes, papayas, oranges, and coconuts, so that the men could enjoy a good supper before they set sail the next morning and have some local fruits to enjoy on the return trip. It was also a good enticement to keep the crew on board, lest they get tempted to go wandering off into town in search of one more night of diversion. Captain Phillips didn't want to take the chance of any of the men getting into trouble in town the night before they were going to leave.

Fortunately—or unfortunately, depending on whose perspective—the most likely candidate to disappear into the Havana night had learned his lesson. In fact, Martin Smith swore off Spanish women after what had happened to him . . . at least for the time being.

While Canady was below deck browning the meat in a dutch oven—a fresh pork butt cut into chunks so that it would cook faster—the men all ate their fill from a sack of bread they were able to buy in the Plaza Vieja at half its usual price, since it was the end of the day. The hearth was almost never used while the men were at sea, so being able to enjoy a hot meal on deck instead of the salt pork and fish that made up their usual rations was a welcome change.

When the meat was nearly done cooking, Canady threw in some chopped-up chayote and carrots, sautéing them in the pork grease over the heat until they were tender. All of the men stood ready with their square wooden plates and piled on heaping servings of the unusual meal.

Once they were served, they all went up on the main deck to eat. It was far too warm and stuffy to enjoy a hot meal down below. The captain said the blessing, and then they all found places to sit and began their impromptu feast.

It was apparent that none of the men had eaten particularly well with all of the excitement of the last couple of days. Each of them was gobbling up whatever was on his plate as though he feared somebody might come along and take it.

Adam ate fast too, but he had never seen chayote before. "What is it?" he asked as he poked it around with his fork.

Martin didn't wait for an answer but instead took a bite of it and then said, "Tastes somethin like some kind of squash or potato, or maybe a cross between the two."

That answer was good enough for Adam. He would've eaten it anyway, of course, but he was curious about the strange little green fruits when he saw them earlier and was skeptical about how they'd be. He worried their flavor would be sweet, like apples, and wondered how they would taste after being cooked in pork grease. He was relieved to know they weren't sweet, but rather they did taste very much the way Martin had described.

Considering how long it took for Canady to cook the meal, it was gone entirely too quick. Nevertheless, the men all had full bellies and were content as they stretched out and breathed in the fresh air as their food digested.

Even better, thanks to clear skies, the men were relieved to know they'd be able to enjoy their last night in Havana sleeping again on the main deck after spending a hot and muggy evening down below because of the torrential downpour of the previous night. And it was a perfect night for it. There was a gentle breeze blowing over the water, and the moon was at its fullest.

"Oy, Fletcher," said Jones. "How are things with your dad?"

"Not so good," Adam replied. "I'd be surprised if he made it through the night."

Jones had been reclining against the rail, but he sat up. "That's awful. What went wrong?"

"I'm not sure. He seemed to be doing alright when he was here—but remember, after Cap'n stitched him up he said that he shouldn't be moved under any circumstances until morning, but—"

"Probably was an infection that set in," interrupted the captain. "That happens right often."

"So you don't think it's just because they moved him too soon?" asked Adam.

The captain tilted his head and appeared to consider the question before he answered it. "Eh . . . It's hard to say. I reckon it could be, but remember I'm no doctor." He too had been reclining, but then he leaned forward and began using his hands to emphasize what he said next. "All I know is that a man can be tough as nails every single day, but when it comes right down to it, his life is fragile. I mean, so many things can cause a fella's condition to fall apart—and fast. I don't really know that it's all that good of an idea to be sittin around now tryin to figure out what went wrong or who's to blame. It won't serve to do a thing in the world but upset you."

Adam threw his head back and looked up at the sky and let out a huge sigh, then lowered his head and looked down at his feet. "You're probably right, but still . . ."

Canady, always one to lighten up the mood, predictably changed the subject. "So any of you fellas get any mementos to take back home?"

"I didn't get a single thing," said Charlie. "I ain't got a wife or babies, so I'm savin my money so I can buy a house. I'm tired of livin with my brother and his family." He tilted his head over towards the captain, then rolled his eyes.

Captain Phillips balled up his kerchief and threw it at his little brother. "Drime! I reckon you will buy a house and move out! That'll be the day! You're tight as a drum, and somehow I can't hardly imagine you forking over money to build a house, much less maintain one."

Charlie grinned. "You go on and keep runnin your mouth, big brother. You'll see. Yes, I'm tight as a drum! How else do you reckon I can save money to get my own place?"

"Well, you just let me know when you're ready for me to

help you move," the captain said, trying hard not to laugh while looking around at the other men, who were all chuckling.

"I sure will. You can be sure of it," said Charlie.

"Alright, settle down, you lot," said Jones. "We can only take but so much of your brotherly love."

"That's right, boys," said Canady. "It's all fun and games now, but in a minute y'all will be fightin, I know it."

The others nodded and chuckled. It was the way with brothers—to poke at each other in a humorous way, that is until one of them pushed it too far and it got awkward for everybody.

"So how 'bout you, Willis?" Canady asked. "You find anything good while we were here?"

"Hmm . . . not much. I don't really have anybody back home to get gifts for—well, except my dad. I did get him a pocketknife that had this real nice carved handle, and I got us both a box of cigars."

Jones threw up his hand. "Me too. That's what I got—some cigars and a couple bottles of some high-quality rum."

The others were impressed. Apparently, no one else had thought of that.

"You shouldn't have told us that, *mate*," Martin teased. "I reckon we'll have that liquor of yours polished off before we make it as far north as Florida."

Jones gave him a cocky grin. "I'd like to see you try that one."

"I'm aggravated now," said Adam. "I was so busy gettin kidnapped and seein my father get shot and all, I never made it out shopping."

"Oh, you're ridiculous," Jones laughed. "I reckon you were too busy to go shoppin, but on the bright side you ended up findin your dad after eighteen years. That's got to be worth somethin."

Adam smiled and nodded. "That's true."

Martin thought for a moment and then said, "Hey, if you hurry up at with your grandmother in the morning, maybe we can swing by the plaza for five or ten minutes. It's so close to here." He looked at Captain Phillips as if he was seeking his consent.

"Don't look at me," the captain said. "I agreed when you said you'd be here by nine. I don't care what you do. You just better be here *by nine*. Not a moment later. If you aren't, you'll be in for a whole mess of trouble when you do get back."

"You know what that means then, don't you?" Adam asked Martin.

"What?"

"We better be back here by nine. Didn't you just hear the captain?" Adam laughed.

The small crew continued talking about everything from the local food to the local women, to what they would do when they first got back home, and so forth. After an hour or so, some of them started excusing themselves to go turn in for the night. By eleven they were all either asleep or passed out from drink— well, mostly just Jones.

Chapter Twenty-Three

WHEN ADAM AND Martin arrived back at the Velasquez estate just after sunrise the next morning, they were immediately allowed through the gate and then shown up to the main house by Felipe. Once they were inside, the short Spanish servant, Timoteo, escorted them into the house. The two of them followed him through the palatial home and were taken to the room where Martin and Charlie had been several days earlier. It was Santiago's study.

Isabel was there, sitting in her son's chair, staring out the huge picture window that looked out onto the courtyard. When she saw Adam and Martin enter the room, she turned her attention towards them and smiled.

"I am glad you are here," she said to Adam. "And I see you have brought your friend."

Martin bowed his head as a courtesy and said, "I'm pleased to see you again, ma'am. I didn't get to say it yesterday, but before we left for home I just wanted to apologize for the damage I caused in your house a couple of days ago."

"Thank you. I accept your apology," said Isabel. She gave him a reserved smile. "Now, I do not wish to be discourteous, but I need a moment to speak with my grandson alone, if you would not mind giving us a few minutes."

Martin looked at Adam for an indication as to whether or not he should leave the room. Adam nodded, so Martin smiled and said, "Certainly, ma'am. I'll see myself out."

Once he was out of the room and the door was closed behind him, Isabel invited Adam to sit in one of the chairs in front of the desk.

"My goodness, it still feels strange to say that— 'grandson'—and not just because it is in English." She began to weep. "I never even knew I had a grandson until . . ." She waved her hand and sighed in exasperation. Adam guessed she was probably thinking about everything that had recently happened with her son.

"You haven't said . . . How is my father?" he asked.

"My son is so very strong. He is still holding on to life—if only by a thread—if you can believe it. He is very much the way he was last night. I do not see that there is any improvement, but I think he is just trying desperately not to let go."

Adam swallowed hard. He wasn't sure what to say. He wanted to believe his father might actually have a chance of recovering, but he knew with almost all certainty that he was very near death, and Adam didn't want to be around when it happened. He wanted to honor his father's wishes in that respect.

"Even though I only barely got to know him, I'm still thankful that I found him," said Adam, "and you."

"Yes. Me too," she said. "It means a great deal to me to know that my Santiago's line lives on in his son."

Isabel lowered her head for a moment, as if she was thinking about what to say. "*Mijo*, I know you do not have much time here before you have to return to your ship, so there is something we need to discuss."

Adam nodded. "Alright. That's just fine. What is it?"

"It is a practical matter, but we need to consider the current circumstances. As you already know, my son—your father—is in a terrible state. You know as I do that it seems very unlikely he will recover. I continue to pray for a miracle, but only God knows when exactly his time will be up. The signs we are having here, though, that we can see are saying that he will die."

"I hope you know," said Adam, "I'm praying for him too. I never thought meeting him would happen like it did, but regardless of what happened eighteen years ago—or all the years in between—I will always be grateful for what he did for me here, and I will carry those memories with me always."

"Yes, I believe you will. And I am happy to know that you feel that way. I want you to also know that if I had known he had a son and a wife somewhere in this world, I would have done everything in my power to make him go to you—either to make a home with you there, or to bring you back here. I would never have approved of him leaving you both the way that he did."

"But you know he did it to protect us from Eduardo, don't you?"

"I know this, but I believe there is something that I could have done to help—if only he would have talked to me about it. I never knew my brother-in-law had this . . . this . . . madness."

Adam scratched his temple. He wondered if she did not fully understand *why* Eduardo had threatened Santiago's life. He also wondered if he should say anything about it.

Isabel continued: "I want you to know just because my son made his decisions as he did, you are still his rightful heir if something happens to him, regardless of what Eduardo says. You know he does not have a will, however. He is a young man, of course, and I'm sure he did not consider that something like this would ever happen."

"Well, actually," Adam began, trying to figure out what to say. In reality, he was thinking about the fact that this woman didn't know about her son's will, or what all it said. For now he thought it best to not address it. "You know, to tell you the truth, being an heir is the last thing on my mind right now."

"Perhaps," she said, "but do not be so quick to dismiss your potential inheritance. There is something you will need to consider. You say your name is Adam Fletcher, but you are the child of my son, and he is Velasquez de Leon. Since he does not have a will, in order to inherit you will need to assume his surname, Velasquez. It is of little concern to me what you call yourself in America, but here you must take your father's name. You must call yourself Adam Velasquez."

Adam tilted his head and made a face that indicated his discomfort with the idea. "My father isn't dead yet. You know . . . maybe the best thing to do would be to wait and see if he dies, and if that happens, then you can send some sort of correspondence to let me know. Then we can talk about this. I'm not so sure how I feel about having this conversation right now."

Adam was no fool. He understood that this was a perfectly reasonable conversation to have, but given the circumstances—that Eduardo had insisted Santiago was illegitimate, which would of course implicate Isabel, *and* that Santiago knew about that— Adam really did not want to be the one to tell all of this to his grandmother. He hoped she would take a hint from his reluctance to discuss it and change the subject.

"You are right," she said. "He is not dead yet, but I think it is preferable that you and I have this conversation now rather than me having to try and communicate with you about this via written correspondences to America. We need to discuss your name change, so you can inherit."

Adam wrinkled his brow and sat forward in his chair. He paused for a moment to think about what she was asking him to do and what he wanted to say. On one hand, he still didn't want to confront her with Eduardo's charges of her infidelity to his brother, but on the other hand, he was taken aback by her ability to treat the situation like a standard business transaction.

"I'm sorry. Let me be sure I understand what you are telling me. You want me to change my name so that I can be accepted as my father's son, so that I can inherit whatever it is that I'm supposed to inherit?"

"Well, yes. That is the way it will have to be. Otherwise, it will appear that you are a bastard, and the court will not likely recognize you as his heir if other members of the family wish to contest your inheritance, namely land holdings and property that would go to some of his cousins if he died without a legitimate heir."

"I can't do it," said Adam. "I know I'm his son, and I know that I'm *not* a bastard, but nevertheless I have been Adam Fletcher all of my life. I can't pretend to be somebody now that I'm not, just to get some inheritance."

"It is only when you are here," she said. "You can call yourself whatever you like once you are gone."

"You don't understand," he said. "I don't want to disrespect you in any way, but the fact is that because of problems between him and his uncle, almost nineteen years ago he had to leave my pregnant mother, who was barely eighteen herself, to give birth to me and raise me alone. They decided way back then to hide their marriage, to pretend that it never even happened, and the fact that she was carrying his heir, and all because Eduardo paid men to try to kill her. Do you understand? Eduardo was ready to kill my mother, and I would imagine any other woman my father might have taken the notion to marry, because he was not going to let him have a legitimate heir."

Isabel's eyes grew large. Adam could tell she wanted to say something, but he continued: "My father was ready to give up the Velasquez inheritance to protect our lives. For more than eighteen years, my mother has been called every name you can imagine because the folks back in Beaufort thought she was a woman of loose morals. They didn't believe she was married, because they never saw a husband. And what did that make me? I have been called a bastard more times than I could count."

"Adam, I'm sorry that—"

"Listen," said Adam. "I understand that you hold the balance of this family's estate until you die, except for the part that was already given to my father in your late husband's will. If my father dies, I want it to be clear in your will that you will give what he would have stood to inherit to the children of Eduardo."

"But why?" Isabel sat with her mouth agape, clearly perplexed at his suggestion. "Why would you say that? Eduardo is dead now."

"Yes, he is. Now his sons are without a father, regardless of what a lousy father he may have been. I don't need this family's riches. I never even knew about them, but Eduardo's sons? Who's to say they wouldn't come after me or my family one day out of the same kind of greed that motivated Eduardo?"

"If you are so concerned about what they might think, then I will leave it up to you to give to them as you see fit from the inheritance. In fact, it is fully within my power to transfer the inheritance to you now, while I am still living, if my son has died, but you need to assume his name. Otherwise, it will raise far too many questions, and it will look scandalous."

"I don't think you would need for me to change my name for you to give me property," said Adam. "And anyway, I would just sign it all over to Eduardo's family. I'm trying to make you understand that I don't want it."

"You are being foolish," said Isabel.

"I am not!" Adam insisted. "There will never be a day when I abandon my mother's name."

Isabel's posture stiffened and she raised her eyebrows at his reaction. She pressed her lips together and looked like she was waiting for him to respond.

He said nothing at first, then finally, "I won't do it."

Isabel appeared to be incredulous at Adam's response. "My late husband loved Santiago and was a wonderful father to him. He wanted him to have everything, and he would want the same for his grandson."

"I'm sorry about that, but I won't do it," he said.

Adam thought he was being clever. Maybe if he kept taking this route, she'd leave the subject alone. The last thing he wanted to do was to let Isabel know that Eduardo had been calling her a whore all these years, and that her own son acknowledged Eduardo's accusations in his will—the will she knew nothing about.

"I think you are being stubborn and immature," she insisted.

"Maybe. But I am not going to pretend that I've grown up with the benefit of knowing he was my father or him helping to raise me, regardless of how virtuous his reasons were for leaving."

"You are being unreasonable, *mijo*," Isabel pleaded. "I can assure you that it will make no difference to you or your mother if you do what I ask, but what do you think your mother would say if you walked away from such an inheritance because of your stubborn pride?"

"My mother would understand? Have you forgotten what I just said? Eduardo tried to have her killed!"

"Yes! All the more reason for her to want you to have justice now."

"You don't know my mother," said Adam. "And anyway, even if that were true, I still wouldn't change my name just so I can receive property."

"But why not? It would only be while you are here."

"I'm leaving in a little more than an hour anyway, remember."

"I am sure your master would let you return to take care of this business if he understood everything that was happening."

This tiny old woman was far more stubborn than Adam could have imagined. It was time to try to fend off her insistence using a different tactic. "Are you telling me that if you were in my mother's shoes, you would be alright with your son living a lie just for economic gain?"

Isabel took a deep breath and gazed out of the window again. Finally, she stood from her chair and walked over to look out on the courtyard. Adam wasn't sure if that meant their conversation was over. He thought that it might, so he got up and started walking towards the door.

"*Mijo*, wait." Isabel walked around to the front of the desk and motioned for him to sit back down.

He came over and took a seat. She took the chair that was nearest to him and brought it very close to where he was sitting, and she sat down facing him.

"You see things in a very simple way, but sometimes in life things are very much more complicated than that."

Adam looked at her but said nothing.

"You are leaving soon, and we do not have much time to argue anymore, so to answer your question, yes, I would done so, and I have done so."

"What?" asked Adam, stunned. "I don't understand what you mean." He wondered if she was about to confess to him more specifically what his father had alluded to in his will.

"Sometimes we do not choose to lie," she said. "We choose to hide the truth. Perhaps it is because it is something of which we are ashamed. Or perhaps we are not ashamed, although we should be, but it is not our wish to hurt someone that we love."

Adam wrinkled his brow and shook his head. "What is this about?"

"I want to share something with you—something I have kept a secret for many, many years, but I am hoping by my telling you it will cause you to reconsider what I am asking you to do."

"What is it?"

"When I was a young girl, only about fifteen or so, one of the places my family lived was in Trinidad. My father was a government official, and although there wasn't much of any kind of Spanish colony there at the time, he was a royal appointee, and so that was my home. I met a young Englishman who used to visit our little island when he was sailing here and there in the Caribbean Sea. You could say we became sweethearts, and we fell in love, but nothing was to come of it. My father would not have permitted me to marry someone like him. Yes, he had money, but he was not Spanish, and he had no title or substantial holdings. Still, he would come see me, and we would spend beautiful afternoons together on the beach at my family's estate. Oh yes, we were very much in love, but fate had other plans for us."

"What happened?"

"My father was appointed to a new position here in Havana. At that time I was a couple of years older. There was an older gentleman who had recently lost his wife and only child during childbirth. He was grieving terribly, and my father thought him to be a good and decent man, so he made an agreement with the man that I could be his bride. So we married."

"I don't understand what any of this has to do with me or my father," said Adam.

"My husband, Juan Diego, *que Dios le bendiga*," she said, crossing herself, "was a good man, but he was so grief stricken and fearful after losing his first wife that he was unable to, well, be as a husband to me. He traveled frequently. One of the times he was away, I was surprised that my young Englishman had found me."

Adam's eyebrows raised in surprise.

She continued her story. "He had gone all the way to Trinidad looking for me, but I was not there. The man who had taken over our estate told him we had come to Havana, so he came here and found me. He had been told I was married, but he wanted to see it for himself. You see, he had come into a great deal of money and was hoping that we would be able to finally be together with my father's blessing, but it was too late."

Adam discreetly looked at a clock that was across the room and remembered he had sent Martin out to wait for him.

Isabel must have detected his nervousness about the time and said, "Do not worry, this will not take much longer."

Adam smiled and nodded. "It's alright. I'm listening."

"*Mijo*, I have never told this to another living soul, but when I consider what you have been through in your life and that your father cannot be there for you now, I think you should know this."

This was taking forever. Adam was very interested in what she was going to say.

"You see, this Englishman and I, we created a child together—in a moment of weakness and indiscretion. Not long after my husband returned, it started to become apparent that I was growing big with child. He knew that the babe could not be his, because we had never even consummated our marriage, but to admit that would have brought much shame and embarrassment upon him. Santiago is that child, and he was raised with the understanding that Juan Diego Velasquez de Castillo was his father. Santiago has never known anything different."

You might be surprised, Adam thought.

"For our family, to hide the truth was the only choice we could make, and my son is the rightful heir of everything you see on this estate and much, much more."

"What about your husband?" asked Adam.

Isabel was pensive and nodded slowly. "Juan Diego wanted it to be this way. He was proud to have a son, even if he was not his true father. And just so you know, yes, Santiago did come to know his real father, only he did not realize who he was. I sent Santiago to meet my Englishman—his father—when he first went to America. I told him to seek him out, that he was an old friend, and that he would help him any way he might need it if he told him that he was my son."

Adam began to feel his body shake. He already knew how this story ended. He had heard some of it before, only not Isabel's version of events.

"Santiago's father is your master, Emmanuel Rogers. Emmanuel knew that Santiago was his son, but I pleaded with him to keep the matter a secret, and he promised me that he would, out of his deep love and devotion to me."

"So you're the one!" Adam exclaimed.

Isabel was confused. "What are you talking about?"

"Oh . . . Oh, I can't believe this." Adam shook his head in disbelief. He then explained, "Not long after Emmanuel brought me on as his apprentice, I ended up getting into kind of a mess. It was bad. Anyway, he told me that he wasn't going to send me away, and that he wanted me to succeed no matter what, and that he had made a promise to someone long, long ago, but he wouldn't say anything about what the promise was or who he made it to." Adam smiled. "But it was you!"

Isabel smiled. "Well, I suppose it must have been."

Adam's mind worked quickly. "If Emmanuel is Santiago's father, then that means Emmanuel is my grandfather."

"This is true," said Isabel.

As happy as it made him to know that, Adam still thought of his master and the lonely life he had been living all this time.

He confronted Isabel about it. "You denied Emmanuel the privilege of having his son know that he is his father all because you thought you had good reasons?"

"*Ay, mijo* . . . Emmanuel and I knew that what we had done was wrong. The way we handled everything was the least damaging way possible. You may form whatever opinions you like, but the decisions were not yours to make. But the one I am presenting to you now is. Please let me arrange for you to present yourself as a Velasquez so you can finally position yourself to inherit the estate that has always been intended for Santiago. If I had thought he'd die before he could inherit, I never would have bothered to stay here all this time. I always knew Eduardo resented the fact that Juan Diego bequeathed the family's inheritance to Santiago, but I never understood why."

Adam realized he should now tell her what he knew. "*Abuela*, there's something I should tell you."

"What is it?"

"Evidently, Eduardo has always been aware of the fact that Santiago was not his brother's son. That was why he did not want him to have a legitimate heir, because he never thought it was right that a man who was not a true Velasquez would inherit the family's largest estate holdings."

"How do you know this?" she asked, her eyes filling with tears.

"Eduardo told me himself, but it is also in my father's will."

Isabel's eyes grew large. "What? Santiago has no will. Why are you saying this?"

"He does have a will. My father told me about it a couple of nights ago. He told me to take it to Eduardo and show it to him, that it should stop him from coming after me, but it didn't."

"Where is this will now?"

"I put it back in his wardrobe yesterday, just before Eduardo came in and tried to attack me. It's in the third drawer down."

Isabel shook her head frantically. "What does this will say?"

Adam suspected she worried about its contents and if it might be embarrassing to her. He knew now he ought to tell her, and so he explained what it said. He saw the color leave her face, and she looked horribly worried.

"This will be in the public record," she said. "This will be a scandal. Oh, I would rather die!"

"Just destroy the document, then," said Adam. "He obviously wrote it as a safeguard in case something like this happened and Eduardo was still living, but he's dead now. My mother and I are the only people who he bequeaths anything to in the will. Without the document, if my father dies, everything that was already his will go to you, anyway. It will be up to you, then, if you want to bequeath the items as he requested in your own way, but you won't have to mention any embarrassing pieces of information."

Isabel thought for a moment, then began nodding slowly. "Yes, that is what I will do. I will do that."

Adam continued looking at her, unsure of what to say.

"Why would Santiago put all of that into his will? Why would he not just talk to me about it?"

"I'm guessing he thought it was the only way he could figure out how to turn down the inheritance. Maybe he assumed that he would outlive both you and Eduardo, in which case he could then inherit everything and pass it on to Eduardo's sons without his will ever having to come out in the public record."

Isabel began to weep. "In the end it appears all of this is my fault. Who would ever think that my one indiscretion so many decades ago could have caused so many years of heartache?"

Adam reached out and took her hand to comfort her. "*Abuela*, as painful as life sometimes can be, everything happens for a reason. Just think, Santiago would never even have been born if you had not . . . well . . ."

Isabel dried her eyes with her handkerchief and offered a weak smile at Adam. "And you would not be here."

Adam nodded. "That's right. And I for one am grateful to be here, so even though all of these terrible things have happened, I would never *blame* you. Eduardo was an evil man, driven by greed and anger. *That* is not your fault."

"No," said Isabel. "It is not. But you know, perhaps we should have talked to him about all of this many years ago, my husband and I. You see, Eduardo was not much younger than you when Juan Diego and I were married. My husband was many years older than him—he was the oldest—and there were only sisters between them. Eduardo came to stay with us shortly after we married because their mother died. He was here when Emmanuel came to find me, and although we never acted anything like lovers in front of Eduardo, he must have either spied on us while he was here or found out some other way. If he has know that all this time—carried that around in him, thinking that his brother did not know—I am not surprised he was so angry."

"None of that matters now," said Adam. "It still didn't give him a right to kill anybody. He should have just confronted you or his brother about it if he was so concerned, but he chose the path of violence."

Isabel squeezed his hand and then looked at the clock. "You have to go soon, *mijo*," she said.

He looked over at the clock too and nodded. "I do. I wish we had more time to visit," he said.

"You will have to come back here to visit me again," she said.

"Or maybe you should come visit me. And Emmanuel Rogers."

She cast her eyes downward, ashamed, and said, "No, I am afraid that cannot be."

"Well, if you ever change your mind, I'm sure you'd be welcome."

She stood and motioned towards the door. Adam then stood and started to cross the room.

"I want you to know, I will be praying for a miracle with my father. If he makes it, hopefully I'll hear from him, but even if he doesn't I'm grateful that we have at least had this chance to get to know each other."

"Me too," said Isabel. "I still think you should reconsider giving up all of that inheritance."

Not this again, thought Adam. He wasn't going to spend any more time trying to convince her to drop the subject, but he did have one thing he wanted to say.

"I may not have a fancy life back in Beaufort, but it's home. There isn't a single thing I could possess, here or anywhere, that would make me feel richer than I do just to finally know who my father is, and my grandfather." He reached out and touched her arm. "And you."

Isabel grabbed him and stood on her tiptoes to hug him and plant a kiss on his cheek. "*Lo siento, mijo*. I am sorry that you have had to learn these things in this way, but I am grateful that I was able to meet you—to learn I have a grandson. I hope you will come back to Havana one day in happier times."

He nodded. "Maybe so."

But in his heart Adam didn't even want to think about coming back. He gave his grandmother's arm a squeeze and stooped down to plant a kiss on her cheek, and then he left.

Chapter Twenty-Four

"YOU ALRIGHT?" MARTIN asked Adam as they got farther away from the Velasquez estate on the way back to the *Gypsy*. Isabel had ordered Timoteo to take them back to their ship in the family's coach.

Adam stared out the window of the carriage and considered the question as he took in the Cuban landscape. It was so different from Beaufort, so foreign to him. "All of this . . . it's bittersweet, you know? I found my father. I actually found my father. But only to say good-bye."

"Are you havin second thoughts about leavin? I mean, do you think you should stay here? Wait to see if he recovers?"

Adam shook his head. "No. First of all, Captain Phillips wouldn't let me stick around here, anyway. He already said so, but even still there's no way I'm going to let the *Gypsy* go back to Beaufort without me on it."

Martin tipped his head. "Alright. Well, it's up to you."

"It might sound silly to you, but I promised my mama I'd come back and bring her wonderful gifts. When my father left for Havana, he never came back . . . even though I'll bet she always secretly hoped that he would. I'm not going to do that to her. In fact . . ." Adam pulled out his pocket watch and checked the time. He then opened the little window so that he could speak to the driver of the carriage. "Timoteo! We need to make a stop at the Plaza Vieja."

The driver nodded. "Yes? We go to la Plaza Vieja, then."

The young men were taken to the bustling marketplace. Adam bought several gifts to take back to Beaufort. For his mother he bought a golden locket, inside of which a tiny portrait could be placed. He picked up diverse souvenirs for Valentine, Emmanuel, Boaz, and the rest of his friends back at Rogers's Shipping Company. He also found something special for Laney Martin—a simple necklace and pair of earrings—that he knew she would be surprised to receive.

They returned to the *Gypsy*, where an impatient Captain Phillips was waiting for them. "Y'all are cuttin it mighty close. I was startin to worry you two might've decided to abandon ship"

"No, Captain," said Adam. "Just tying up some loose ends."

"All finished?"

Adam nodded. "I think so."

The captain grinned. "Let's go on back home, then."

"Aye, Captain. I can hardly wait."

Chapter Twenty-Five

"OH! THANK YOU, God!" Adam exclaimed as they approached the Topsail Inlet. He knew he was now just moments away from home sweet home.

As the *Carolina Gypsy* made her way into Taylor Creek, Adam looked through his spyglass and was able to see friends and family of the men on board beginning to run towards the docks where the sloop would be moored. Whenever a local ship would return home from a long voyage, it could be spotted at a distance by folks in town, and everyone would come down to welcome their men back home.

He looked towards the direction of the Topsail Tavern to see if he could see his mother or Valentine or anyone coming towards the docks, but there was no one—at least not that he could make out. He knew he wouldn't see Laney Martin arrive to greet him. She lived around Lennoxville Point, which was too far away to hear the folks in town announcing the *Gypsy*'s return.

Oh well, he thought, *that just means I can surprise 'em when I walk into the tavern.* He tried to push away a worry that something might have happened in the time he had been gone.

He put his spyglass back into his pocket and walked over to stand beside Martin at the rail. Martin had no one who would be waiting for him to return. His parents were both dead, and he was an only child. His only family close by was his cousin Laney.

"Glad to be back home?" asked Adam.

"I am," said Martin.

"Think you'll be up for going on another one of these trips anytime soon?"

"Maybe so, but if we do, no adventures, alright?"

Adam laughed. "Agreed. I think I've had enough adventure to last a right good long while."

As the *Gypsy* was being brought about into position in front of Rogers's warehouse, the dockworkers were standing by to help off-load the vessel. Adam's heart raced as he looked inside the giant cargo doors of the building and saw a staid Emmanuel standing there, his hands clasped in front of him. *Is something wrong? Why is he standing like that? He looks worried,* Adam thought. He tried to push out of his mind the multitude of reasons why Emmanuel might wear such an expression, but there was no need. He soon was able to make out a smile spreading across the old man's face. Apparently, he had just been waiting until he was able to put his eyes on his young apprentice.

The next several minutes were a blur, with dockworkers hurriedly helping set the ramp and assist with the unloading of the vessel. Once Adam was finally able to disembark, he ran down the ramp and over to Emmanuel and surprised the old man by grabbing him in a manly hug.

"What's this?" said a bewildered but bemused Emmanuel.

"I'm so glad to be home," said Adam. "We have a lot to talk about."

"Oh?"

"We do. About my father . . . And Isabel."

Emmanuel's eyes grew very big. Then he nodded and smiled at Adam. "I see. Well, I suppose we do have much to talk about, then. But perhaps you should first go and see your mother."

"She's alright, isn't she?"

"Of course, my boy, but she's been so worried, what with the ship being delayed and all."

Adam nodded in understanding. "Alright, I'll go over there in a little bit, but first I need to tell you something important."

"What is it?"

"Can we go upstairs and talk?"

"You sure you don't want to run over to the tavern first?"

"I'm sure," Adam insisted.

"Very well," said Emmanuel.

He went over and gave a few instructions to Boaz Brooks, then walked on ahead and motioned for Adam to follow him upstairs to the living quarters. As Adam got to the top of the stairs and reached the balcony, he breathed in deep. He remembered that first time he came to the warehouse the year before, just at the start of his apprenticeship, and how the place looked so big from up there. It still smelled of the warm fragrances of tobacco, rum, and cedar shingles.

When they entered the main room of the living quarters, Adam looked around and was thankful to be back home. He never did get so used to living there that he took for granted the exotic furnishings and decor that reflected Emmanuel's lifetime of collecting wares from around the world.

"Well, set your bag down and take a seat," said Emmanuel. "Want me to make some tea?"

Adam shook his head. "No, I'm not going to stay that long right now. I just wanted to let you know about something before you heard it from someone else."

"You'll be the death of me, boy," Emmanuel remarked, making his way around to sit in his favorite chair and motioning for Adam to sit on the settee next to it. "This must be of great importance for you to be so solemn. What on earth is the matter?"

"My father, Captain Velasquez, he was gravely injured. He may already be dead."

Emmanuel's face fell. "What? What is this all about? What in the world has happened down there?"

Adam proceeded to tell Emmanuel about how he had gone off in search of Alonso Cordova and ended up getting kidnapped instead. Then he explained how Santiago got involved in the search and what all had happened, including the gunfight in which he took a severe hit.

"He did it to protect me," said Adam. "I know now who he is."

Emmanuel took a very deep breath and appeared to be fighting the urge to weep. "He's your father, Adam."

"Yes, he is."

"He told you?"

"He did."

"How did he know?"

"He figured it out when he was talking to Martin and

Charlie, and they mentioned my mother's name. They told him that she'd kill them if they didn't find me."

"Mary Fletcher. Yes. Of course he'd remember her name." Emmanuel looked reflective.

"You knew he was my father, didn't you?"

Emmanuel nodded.

"And you're my grandfather."

At that, Emmanuel could not restrain himself anymore. He gripped his handkerchief and brought it to his cheek as he began to sob. "That I am," he said. "How on earth did you find out?"

"Isabel told me—my grandmother. There's a lot more to all this mess, but I can explain all of that to you later. The important thing is now I know."

Emmanuel said nothing. He just nodded. He was very emotional.

"And you've always known this?" Adam raised his eyebrows in concern. "Why haven't you told me?"

The old man finally composed himself. "That is a fair question. Do you remember when we had that talk last year, and I told you I had made a promise to someone long, long ago and that I had a vested interest in your future?"

Adam nodded. "I do. You were talking about Isabel, weren't you?"

Emmanuel nodded. "I promised her when our son—Santiago, your father—was just a wee babe that I would never reveal the truth to anyone. She asked me to make that promise."

"And you just went along with it?"

"I didn't have much of a choice."

"I disagree," said Adam.

"Well, you are entitled to disagree, but I chose the least

destructive path I could. I thought in this way the only one who would suffer would be me."

Adam took a deep breath and looked across the room, staring out the window at the ships in Taylor Creek. "And you never would have told me?"

Emmanuel shook his head.

"Never?"

"No. I would have taken that secret to my grave, just as I promised her I would, but I'd be lying if I didn't tell you what a tremendous relief it is to me that you now know the truth—all of it."

"I've had a lot of time to think about this on the trip back home, and there's one thing I wonder," said Adam.

"What's that, son?"

"If you knew all this time that I was your grandson, why did you never try to meet me or get to know me before you took me on as an apprentice last year?"

Emmanuel looked like he was pondering how he would answer the question. He sighed and said, "I've always had an eye on you, my boy. I never once questioned your mother's love for you and her ability to raise you up well."

"How did you even know about my mother and father? From what I heard, they didn't really tell anybody. Only Valentine knew."

Emmanuel tipped his head forward. "Let me explain. When Santiago first came here and explained that he was the son of Isabel and Juan Diego, I knew he had to be my son. I knew she must have sent him to me."

Adam listened intently.

"Well, I admit that I always kept a close eye on him after that. I knew, for instance, that he had taken a room there at the tavern. I also knew that he stayed around here in Beaufort much longer than he needed to, and there must've been something keeping him here. I knew who your mother was, of course. I also knew that later that summer he was gone, but her belly was growing. I asked Valentine about it one day, and he only told me that she had eloped with a sailor from Cuba, but that after the Spaniards attacked the town, he ran him off. I was suspicious of his story, of course, but I felt sure that he was referring to my son. I never told him that, though."

"How did you know it was your son and not one of the other sailors on his vessel?"

Emmanuel laughed. "My son was the most handsome one, of course! And he was also the only one who took a room at your tavern. It didn't take much for me to put two and two together. And then after you were born and as you started growing, my suspicions were confirmed. You looked so much like your father."

Adam smiled and looked away. "Everybody was saying that down in Havana. I never noticed it until somebody pointed it out."

"Well, you look very much like your mother. You've got her smile for sure, and she has dark features as well, but that wavy hair and those eyes . . . Those are your father's. And I want to tell you something else: I also have known Valentine since before even your mother was born, and I'm sure he knew that I knew your father, since I had done business with him while he was here. Valentine always knew I would ask about you and I would offer to help financially if there was ever any need for it, but of course you know Valentine. He's far too proud to take any help."

Adam nodded. "That he is. Still, I don't understand why you never tried to get to know me earlier."

"The reason why I never tried to make your acquaintance before I took you on as an apprentice is because quite honestly I think it would have been too difficult for me. That's a poor excuse to you, I'm sure, but it's the truth. I told you I intended to keep my promise to Isabel, but knowing you personally as a little boy, watching you grow up and being in your life—well, it would have made it very hard to keep that promise. You are my grandson, after all." At that, Emmanuel got choked up again.

Adam rose from his seat on the settee and stood so he could hug Emmanuel in his chair. "Well, thank God we don't have to worry about keeping secrets anymore."

"Indeed," said Emmanuel. He composed himself quickly and patted Adam on the shoulder. "You hurry over to the tavern now and go see your mother. She's been worried to death about you since the *Gypsy* left Taylor Creek. She might've even sprouted a few gray hairs as a result of it!"

Adam chuckled. "Alright. I'm going now."

He started to leave but then turned back. "Everything will be different now. You know that?"

Emmanuel smiled. "I do."

ADAM WANTED TO RUN almost the whole way back to the Topsail Tavern. Now that he had told Emmanuel what he knew, he would be glad to see his mother and put her fears to rest, and to see Valentine and tell him all about his adventures in Cuba.

He could hear music coming from the tavern before he even got inside. It was a welcome surprise, since Valentine had temporarily banned hiring musicians a couple of years earlier after a bar fight broke out between sailors from two different ships over which song the musicians should play. In the two years since, the only time the Topsail had music was when a patron happened to come in with a fiddle or a guitar, which didn't happen often.

Thanks to the heat on this bright and sunny Saturday, the heavy oak door to the tavern was propped open with a brick, and all the windows were open. Adam wondered if anyone inside would spot him before he stepped across the threshold.

As it happened, when he came through the door of the tavern, everything was exactly the way he left it—with the exception of the lively tune that was being played, of course. Valentine was sitting in his usual spot behind the bar, and tavern patrons were eating, drinking, and making merry.

Adam stood there for a moment just to take it all in. When Valentine looked up and noticed it was him, he strode over to the bar to greet him.

"Welcome home, son," said the ruddy-complected, middle-aged barkeep. He walked around the bar to shake Adam's hand.

"I'm happy to be back," said Adam. "I've got plenty to tell you about, but I've gotta see Mama first. Is she here?"

"In there." Valentine tipped his head back towards the kitchen and smiled.

Adam walked past the bar and then pushed open the door to the kitchen and saw his mother getting some plates piled high with food to take to some hungry customers.

"Hey, Mama," he said as he stood near the doorway, smiling.

Mary looked as if she was so focused on what she was doing that it took her a couple of seconds to register her son's voice. As soon as she did, she put the plates down on the huge butcher-block table in the middle of the kitchen and ran over to hug her son.

"Oh, thank you, Jesus, thank you, Jesus, thank you, Jesus," she said over and over again, holding her son tightly and crying tears of joy. "I was so afraid you wouldn't come back."

"Mama!" said Adam in an attempt to comfort her. "Why in the world would you worry that I wouldn't come back?"

She held him out at an arm's length so she could get a good look at him. "You look alright, healthy and all . . . Oh thank you, Jesus!"

"I thank Jesus too, Mama, but you didn't need to worry so much. I promised you I'd be back, and here I am."

"Yes you did," she said, grinning at him as though she was in utter disbelief.

"And I promised you I'd bring you back gifts." He reached into the little sack he had brought with him from the warehouse and handed her the locket he had bought for her on the day he left Havana. As she held it in her hand and admired it, he said, "I have you a few other things too, but I wanted you to have this first."

"Oh, it's beautiful!" she exclaimed. "But it looks so expensive! How could you afford this?"

She put it around her neck and looked inside.

Adam didn't answer. He just smiled at her.

"Oh, look! There's a tiny portrait of you inside!" She marveled at the likeness.

"Believe it or not," said Adam, "that was painted by a fellow on the *Gypsy*—Ed Willis. He's a real good artist and did a lot of that to pass the time on the way back."

"You shouldn't have, you know," she said. "I'm sure this cost way too much." She gave him a jokingly stern look. "But I'll always treasure this." She hugged him again.

"Let me fix you something to eat," she offered.

"I'd love that."

Mary delivered the plates she had prepared earlier to the customers in the dining room, then came back into the kitchen to fix something for Adam to eat. As she did, Adam told her all about the sea voyage, how he didn't get sick, and how beautiful it was down in the Caribbean, but he didn't say one word about what had happened to him in Cuba. And he wasn't sure that he would.

He knew he'd have to tell her at some point that he had finally met his father, and also that he had learned Emmanuel was his grandfather. Nevertheless, he figured he would spare her the details of his ordeal with the kidnappers.

Adam knew that he would tell Valentine all about what had happened . . . eventually. Not today, though. Today he was just glad to be back home.

<<<<>>>>

Acknowledgements

AS ALWAYS, MY GRATITUDE, first and foremost, goes to God for allowing me to write and publish another novel. I'd also like to express my appreciation to Capt. Horatio Sinbad of the *MEKA II*, as well as to research historian and author Kevin Duffus, for offering their historical and technical expertise relating to tall ships and eighteenth century seafaring. Additionally, I want to thank Marcus Trower for his brilliant copy editing and great advice in the early stages of revising this novel. Finally, I want to thank all of you who read *The Smuggler's Gambit* and expressed your enthusiasm for its sequel. I hope this new adventure was worth the wait.

—S.D.G.—

READ THE WHOLE SERIES

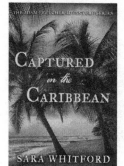